Love, Story

Thomas Cannon

Published by Thomas Cannon, 2023.

LOVE, STORY

First edition. October 30, 2023.

Copyright © 2023 Thomas Cannon.

ISBN: 979-8223200680

Written by Thomas Cannon.

Chapter 1 This Old House

Wes, with his hog-hair number one in hand, stared at his latest painting. He wondered if it didn't look right because of its departure from his normal style or that he was in one of his moods. He was going off a simple sketch he had made, but he remembered the Chicago skyline at sunset. Glowing orange and red behind cold skyscrapers, the sky had moved him to capture its beauty. A beauty destined to fade and be replaced with the night sky, but never duplicated. A beauty that held and dispersed all sadness.

Sally whistling the strip tease song, danced into the room. She pulled down a strap from her tank top and swung her hips into his side.

"Do you like my dance?" she asked.

"What?"

She leaned forward and gave him a sideways glance inviting him to look down her top. "Do you like my little dance?"

"Sure." He turned the picture to re-center it in the afternoon light coming through the dormers. "Very funny."

She glided her arm around his neck and blew lightly in his ear. He shrugged and jerked his head to one side. Besides trying to shrug off her intrusion on his concentration, Wes didn't like the way her sleeper hold reminded him of the three inches she had on him.

"You going to be much longer?"

"I've finally gotten the right tone of gray glaze here. I have to paint until I finish in case I can't get it back."

"So, like ten minutes?"

"I think you're serious about that." Wes watched her stroll across the room and do an isolated twirl so quick her black-haired ponytail became perpendicular to her head, and she landed in a stance facing him.

"I'm bored, and the dog needs to go out."

"Two problems that solve each other." Wes held his brush in his mouth like a tango dancer with a rose while he adjusted his painting to block the view of his wife. "You know you could, at least, look at my paintings."

"I can't. Your dog has to go pee."

WES CAME DOWN THE STAIRS from his studio over the garage. "I rushed it. Painting the glaze." He looked over to Sally slouched on the couch with her feet planted on the coffee table. She was snapping her gum and reading a magazine.

"You've been up there long enough to glaze three paintings. Meanwhile, I've begun making the emotional preparations for my prediction to come true."

"Oh." He sat down on the recliner in front of him and crossed his legs. "Have you thought of some physical preparations of supper? It's your night."

"On our wedding night, I told you that you would leave me on our ten-year anniversary because you would be rich and successful." She flipped back to the front of the magazine and began flipping through it again. "And our ten-year anniversary is coming up."

"In three months, Sally." He pinched the bridge of his nose.

"Ten weeks. See isn't that prophetic? Ten weeks before our ten-year anniversary, I repeat the prediction."

"No. It's weird and stupid. Just as it was when you announced it the first time in the middle of sex."

"We were already living together. I wanted to make our honeymoon special."

"I should have left you right then and there."

Sally closed the magazine. "Why? Why would you say that? How could you say that?"

"I'm kidding."

"You didn't sound like you were kidding."

Wes glanced around the room for the TV remote. Sally was the TV watcher and Wes assumed she had let the remote slip down between the couch cushions. He looked at her as she glared at him. Whatever it took to get her unhurt by his joke, he didn't have. He mustered what he could. "Well, I was."

"You've been on my mind all day and now you act like a jerk."

Don't blame me, I didn't put me there, he thought. He was also wishing he thought about her often too. However, when he worked, he was completely absorbed in his painting. Knowing what a husband should do (from reruns of Everybody Loves Raymond), he lied. "I always think of you." He did think of her sometimes though. When he painted a beach at sunset or the knees on a little girl.

"What will you think about after you leave me?"

He shook his head. "I'm tired, Sally. I've been working since six this morning."

"I worked today, too, you know. We have a big order of two table sets we have to finish by next Thursday."

"And are you tired?"

"No. More antsy, actu-"

"Then why bring it up?"

"Because it's because of my shop that you get to paint all day."

"So, write me up a bill and I'll pay you back." He stuffed his hands down the cushions of his chair fishing for the remote. He pulled up some lint, a pen, and some change. "Here. Some good faith money."

"I don't care that I support us."

"Again. Then why bring it up?" Wes was teasing and yet his comments were taking a hard edge. He enjoyed banter with a hard edge, but Sally could not. Somehow, he expected her to learn to like it. Even after ten years of not.

"God. You're such a jerk." She tossed her magazine on the coffee table, but it slid along the other magazines on it and hit the floor.

"Then you shouldn't care that I'm going to leave you. Did you pick up those canvases for me?"

"Why would I want to help you become successful and leave me?"

Wes picked up her magazine from the floor. "So, you didn't do that one small thing I needed you to do?"

"I forgot." Both looked over to the dog as he whimpered by the front door. "Bobvila, I need to take you out." She picked up her apple.

"Bobvila still needs to pee?" Wes got up and jammed his feet into the sandals he kept by the back door. "You need to take care of your dog, Sally."

"He's yours. I bought him for you."

"You always say that. You can't keep saying that when you know I'm allergic. It'd be like buying a family of blind people lawn darts."

"They don't make lawn darts anymore."

"And if he's my dog, then why did you get to name him?"

"You would have named him Picasso or something."

Wes sighed. "He needs to go out at least four times a day."

"You know," she said, "for an artist, you're not much of a free spirit."

Chapter 2 Kid-ing

WES DECIDED THE OVERCAST skies darkening his studio was a good excuse to knock off early and spend some time with Sally. He came downstairs and stood in the doorway of the kitchen as Sally stacked up toasted cheese sandwiches from the griddle onto a plate. He cocked his head and walked toward her. "There must be eight1 sandwiches there and more cooking. How hungry are you?"

"There for Danton, Tad, and Phyllis."

"Tonight? The last thing I need is those hellions running around here. When are they getting here?"

Sally pointed her cheesed spatula over his shoulder and out the open patio door. "Twenty minutes ago."

"Hi, Uncle Wes," Danton said with a grin, looking over the screen of his portable video game.

"What's a hellion?" Phyllis asked.

"Someone from hell," Tad answered, pitching stones from the landscaping at the back fence. His chubby face red from the exertion.

"What's hell? Maybe I want to go. Sometimes Mommy tells Trudy to go there."

"It just means troublemaker." Wes said.

Phyllis looked up at him. She was cute with her mess of dark curly hair and dark eyes blinking up at him. Like her brothers, she bore a strong resemblance to Nancy. Even at four, Phyllis had a meaty build like her mother. "Do I make trouble, Uncle Wes?"

"Sally." Wes turned from the kids and looked at her. "Help me."

"Don't you like us?"

Sally took the plate of sandwiches through the screen door. "It's not you, Phyllis. It's Uncle Wes. If being good with kids was artistic, he'd be great at it, but it's not."

"Sally. I'm good with kids."

"As natural as using a Phillips screwdriver on a hex head."

"What on a what?"

"Go get some ketchup for the kids."

"Ketchup? For toasted cheese?"

"See, Wes, you don't understand children."

WES WATCHED THE KIDS grease their sandwiches with ketchup and stuff them into their mouths. He couldn't believe there wasn't any talking, any pleasantries, just hyenas over a kill. Then they scampered away from the patio table to watch TV inside while their ketchup crusted over on their plates.

He glanced over at Sally eating a toasted cheese with two hands while he worked at his sandwich with a knife and fork. "When your business expands, we'll have to get a bigger house."

"What does that mean?" Sally said shooting him a look and a crust out of her mouth.

"It means a house with more-"

"Shut up. Tell me why you'd say that."

"Because whenever your employees have a problem, you end up rushing to help. Lately that has meant turning our home into a daycare."

"Trudy and Nancy are my friends."

"Why are their kids over here?"

"Because I like them over here, Wes. I'm their Auntie Sally. Plus, they set their last babysitter on fire. It wasn't Tad's fault, though."

"Doesn't matter."

"The babysitter wasn't even hurt."

"DOESN'T MATTER."

"What does matter is that Trudy and Nancy are my friends. Not just my employees. They are going to couples therapy to work some things out and then hopefully out to dinner. Okay, Wes?"

Wes sighed. "You know I like them. But I was thinking about last night and your prediction. I'm going to spend more time with you."

"We can still have a nice night." It was at that moment the three kids ran from the living room and surrounded them.

"Dessert. Dessert. Dessert. Dessert," they chanted. Wes gathered up their dinner plates and took them to the sink.

After ice cream, Wes took Bobvila for a walk. He tried to pry the kids away from The *Smokey and The Bandit* movie Sally always showed them, but then went alone. He took his time and when he got back, the house was quiet.

Until he heard screaming from his studio.

The three kids were chasing each other around his easel with pillows. Scattered on the floor were masks made from paper plates and his expensive paint.

"All right," he yelled. "Enough."

The kids froze in their tracks.

"Who started this? I want to know."

The kids immediately pointed at him. Then he noticed they were actually pointing behind him to Sally standing on a chair and about to hit him with a couch cushion.

"You wouldn't dare," he said to her.

"You're right." She stepped down and sidled to the center of the room. "I wouldn't." She picked up a palette of paint they had been using for their masks. "But I would do this." Sally took a glob of green paint and painted a mustache on him. "There."

Wes looked to Sally's raised eyebrow and then to Phyllis who was giggling. He plucked a paint palette from one of the boys. "Oh yeah? Is that funny little girl?" he asked, painting a yellow mustache on her.

While he was doing that, Sally put her hand in paint and slapped it on his fresh canvas. Wes smeared the paint on his palette onto his hand and slapped his hand on Sally's butt. When the two boys laughed, Sally mushed their mouths with her paint gobbed hands.

Okay, you vandals," Wes said, squinting at them. "As long as your ringleader has ruined my canvas, you are going to use it to make a masterpiece."

"I love it, Wes," Sally said. "Let's do it."

The boys were through showering, and watching TV when Wes came to stand in the doorway while Sally washed Phyllis's hair in the bathtub. "Wes baby, you know how to throw a party."

"It was you, Sally. You're good with small people."

"Children, Wes. Why are you so afraid of the word?"

"It's going to sting my eyes." Phyllis looked up at Sally.

Sally turned her attention to the girl's sudsy hair. "No, it won't, honey. Aunt Sally won't let it." She took a dry washcloth, put it over Phyllis's eyes, and held it there. "Put your noggin back."

Wes watched as Sally dumped water over Phyllis' head and massaged the suds out. As she concentrated on pouring more water through the slick hair, he couldn't think of a time that Sally looked happier.

This made him angry because that included when they were making love. Still, he didn't want to ruin the beautiful moment for her.

"Sally, you have to get fresh water." Wes didn't want to ruin the moment. He couldn't, however, stop himself. "You just can't rinse her with the water she's sitting in."

"Why not. It's just little girl water."

"Because you just can't, and the water is pretty murky with paint."

"Fine." She turned the water on and as Phyllis stood, fidgeting in anticipation of the water, Sally tried to get her to put her head back and wasn't successful.

When Phyllis cried, Sally shot him a look.

Soon enough though, Phyllis was wrapped in a big towel and sitting on Sally's lap in the living room. "I hope they work things out," Wes said.

"Not now," Sally rested her cheek on Phyllis's warm wet head.

Wes wondered how many nights and how many ruined canvasses there would be, but he felt good when Trudy and Nancy came and got freshly bathed kids. Also going home with them was a large canvas with a combination of finger-painting; handprints; crudely drawn Pokémon's; Wes's abstract representation of loss of innocence through racism in the Lion King; and Sally's stick figure family.

Chapter 3 For Love or Money

Wes was just about to melt into sleep when he felt Sally's hand slide over his thigh. They were still in a naked, after-love-making embrace and he opened an eye to look at her. Sometimes when he opened his eyes, her big dark eyes were open and staring back at him only inches away. Now, she appeared to be asleep; her breathing even. Then she moved her hand closer to business and there was no question she was awake.

"Come on, Sal."

She snuggled up to him, putting her chin on the top of his head. "Wasn't it so good the first time?"

Must not have been for you, he thought. "Wonderful." The word made her zero in on her target. "Hey. I got a lot on my mind. I'm really worried about my gallery opening."

"The only thing you should be about having your own show is excited. So, what you're saying is you would rather lay there and worry than make love to me and not have to think about it?" She gestured with her hand as she talked as if she was a pastor and his crotch her pulpit.

It's because I would be thinking about it all along, Wes thought. He pictured how upset she would be if he wasn't able to show his appreciation for her a second time. "I'm pretty tired."

She was gone. She had retreated to facing the wall. "Come on, Hon," he said. "Don't be like this. You don't understand because you don't even like my art."

"Yes, I do. I think you're as good as Norman Rockefeller."

"That's not a compliment. In many, many different ways."

"That's who you try to imitate don't you? You do it good. Everyone says so."

"You mean Norman Rockwell for one. For two, my themes and tones are the opposite of his. You know nothing about my life's work."

"You do know right, I'm naked and you're discussing art? While I'm naked."

Chapter 4 Back to the gray

Wes had the glaze scraped off the canvas and was working to get his right tint of gray back when he heard the front door shut. It jarred him to realize it was already time for Sally to leave for work. He tried to go back to the gray, but the thought that Sally was still upset nagged at him. He set down his brushes and picked up his coffee cup to go get a refill.

In the kitchen, Sally sat at the large kitchen table she built for their first anniversary. "I knew it. You wait until I leave for the shop and then come downstairs."

"I lost track of time until I heard the door. I was really-" He looked at her in her denim shirt, her hair in a ponytail pulled through an old Cubs hat and her work gloves on the table in front of her. "Did you take the dog out this morning?"

"Didn't you?"

"At six, Sally. You have to take him out before work in case I get busy."

"You paint. Your agenda can't get too full. But I never know what I will face when I get to work."

"Then why are you sitting there when you'll be late?"

"Why did you wait until you thought I left before coming downstairs?"

He sat down in the chair across from her. It was the first time they had sat together at the table since she had brought it home. It was a shiny black table with long tapered legs like a racehorse and it did not fit in with their brown, outdated kitchen. For a moment, he pictured

13

stripping off her clothes and making love on the table like they did in their first apartment. "Well, why didn't you come up and say good-bye to me?"

She stood up. "Because you tell me I'm interrupting you when I do that." She picked up her gloves, muttering, "I think I'll be glad when you leave me."

Wes heard the front door slam and Sally rev her pick-up. Before he got to the coffee pot for his coffee, the phone rang. It was Sally on her cell. "You're coming to my volleyball game tonight, right?"

Chapter 5 Marriage is like the seasons- you get four of them.

Sally sat with her crew around a big worktable as they ate their sack lunches. Rocking on her stool, she chewed on her turkey sandwich and stared at Nancy. Tall redheaded Nancy in her typical flannel shirt with the arms cut off. "No, I don't think I'm a dork for telling him my prophecy."

"No, you misunderstood me, Sally. I think you're a dork for believing it."

"I don't want to live a lie. You know what I mean?"

Trudy pointed her finger and swallowed the tomato from her salad. "Before dating me, Nancy lived with her husband for nine years and had three children. She knows about living a lie."

"And it sucking," Nancy followed. "And me not sucking."

Tiffany and Ellie, the two high school girls that worked part-time giggled.

"Sorry girls," Nancy said. "Fact of life. That's all men think about."

"Wes doesn't think about that stuff all the time. I wished he did more often." Now Trudy giggled. Sally shrugged her shoulders. "It makes me feel sexy sometimes. My dad doesn't think about sex all the time."

"Where is your dad?"

"He's out eating in his truck."

"Doesn't he like us?" Trudy bit her mini carrot in half.

"He's listening to a religious station," Ellie giggled again.

"It's reruns of Rush Limbaugh," Sally said. "Just because he listens, doesn't mean he believes everything Rush said."

"Not a dildo head?" Nancy scoffed.

"You mean ditto-head."

"I know what I said."

"My dad is not prejudiced. He taught me to be a thinking person. To show some sophistication." She up-ended her family-sized Doritos bag and let the crumbs avalanche into her mouth. "But he taught me to be strong, too."

"Maybe too strong," Nancy said. "You've helped out every one of us in this room a thousand ways. However, men, and Wes is one, need to be needed. If you're self-sufficient, then they can't feel like they are the protector. That's not just my lesbianess talking. Even Tiffany and Ellie know it."

The girls tittered. Ellie looked at Tiffany. "Tiffany's boyfriend is building her a nightstand in shop class."

"He knows you work at a furniture factory, right?"

Tiffany smiled. "No."

"Wes is different. He used to paint for me. I didn't understand his paintings when he was done, but they were for me. It was the best feeling anyone ever had and that's all I want now."

Trudy gathered up her paper bag and corralled her crumbs with her hand. "From what I see from my brothers, men are more comfortable with marriages as they progress, and women get upset it's not the same as when they first get married."

Sally sat for a moment. It was spring in Chicago. One of the first days of having the large overhead doors open. They only opened out into the alley, but to Sally there wasn't a more pleasant place to be. "Marriage is like the seasons," she said. "It starts out like spring. When things are new, it just makes you happy to see everything start. Like now, we have a nice breeze blowing in here. But by the summer, it gets hot and muggy and we sweat like pigs as we work. Then it's winter and we have to wear long johns and work faster just to generate a little body heat. Not as great as spring, but I still love it.

"Men are not like that though. As soon as it gets uncomfortable, they want to call it quits. They have to futz with the fans and the furnace and-"

"Wes is a good guy," Trudy said. "And your dad didn't do that. So where did you get such a batty theory? You seem like the one tinkering with something working just fine."

"No," Sally shook her head. "Something's wrong. Even though it sounds, looks, and feels like nothing's wrong. And if his shows are as successful as I think they will be, it's going to get worse."

Chapter 6 Into the volley

Wes bought a bottle of Compari and slunk up to a pub table out by the volleyball court mid-way through Sally's game. He was just in time to see a well-built guy on her team give her a celebratory bear hug that lifted her off the ground. Wes compared his own short, thin, un-toned body to the guy groping his wife. He corrected himself. *The guy now being groped by my wife,* he thought as he watched her wind up and slap him on the butt. *And muscle head and Sally are basically the same height.*

She got set as one of her teammates served the ball. *She's too angular in the face,* Wes told himself. At the same time, he saw her beauty. Her strong, tan legs planted firmly in the sand. Her wide smile of teeth and freckled face devoid of any make-up. Her ponytail bobbing in anticipation of action. He could not look away from her. The ball was served, passed around by the other team and hit away from her, yet she still exploded into motion and kept her eye locked on the ball.

The recipient of Sally's butt slap hit the ball to a guy in front with a barbed wire tattoo around his medium-size bicep, but Sally stepped in front of him and spiked the ball.

Wes watched as the other team returned it, making Sally dive for it and bump it off the back of her hand as she landed in the sand. He knew there was a term for that but before he could Google it on his phone so he could call it good to Sally after the game; he was distracted by the guys next to him.

"Wow, look at that chick go."

"Who?"

"The chick with the rack."

"Sally? Yep she's awesome."

"I gotta get me some of that."

"Dude, her husband is right there."

"No, that's Wes Story. Remember in high school, he always had some art crap up in the lobby? He's gay."

"Oh, yeah. But I'm telling you that's her husband."

"Look at her now. Her team's going to win on her spikes alone. And Wes was in that gay rights club- DECA."

"That's a business club, dumbass."

"Same thing. Look at her. She's a frickin' Amazon."

AFTER THE GAME, SALLY made her way over to Wes, but was stopped by 'slapped my wife on the butt' guy. "You rocked out there, Sally."

"Thanks Curtiss. You too."

The jerk from the next table was instantly standing there making a trio with them. "Hey, Curtiss. You played awesome. Who's your friend here?"

Curtiss looked the jerk over. "This is Sally. Sally, this is guy who I played pool against last Friday."

"Hi. Sally. Can I get you two some refreshment after your hard-fought game?"

"Refreshments? Hard-fought game? Now, who's flamboyant?" Wes muttered to himself and got up. In his best lisp, he said, "Excusse me, boyz. Can I steal Sally away here for a little girl talk? Poopers, but it's important. I'll be done with her by the time you get back with her drinky-poo."

Sally sat down so Wes was taller than her as he stood. She knew he liked that. "Why do that?"

"I wanted your attention while someone else paid for your drinks tonight. You know, I came down here for you and you're chatting those meatheads up. Well, I guess those two are here for you too, but I had better things to do."

"Then go do them."

He looked at her as she leaned on the table and put her hand on the back of her neck. "I didn't mean it like that. I was just trying to be funny instead of upset."

She looked down at his brown loafers. She had known other artists. Bohemians who walked around barefoot, bare-chested, and in ratty jeans. She found it strange now to have been attracted to Wes's thin legs and ever-tucked-in shirt. However, she couldn't imagine her life without his boyish features and narrow body. Actually, she had already imagined it and was already missing him. "You're the only one I want to be here for me," she said with an honesty that shook him.

Still, what came out of his mouth was, "Then why did you grab that guy's butt?"

"What? It's a sports thing. Didn't you ever see that on football?"

"You know on Sundays I watch NASCAR. If there isn't a good exhibit at the museum."

Sally laughed. "Let's just go home, Wes. And be together."

This is her element, he thought to himself. Her wanting to go home made him want to stay for her. *This is her fun and her glory.* So instead of getting up, Wes nodded over her shoulder. "We can't. The drink in Curtis' hand isn't going to drink itself."

Chapter 7 Print Rack Envy

Wes led Juan, Amanda, and Saul up the stairs to show them his studio. The room was why Wes had chosen the house. It had a large dormer overlooking the backyard and two large skylights. Wes imagined it had been a children's playroom because it was light and airy and the realtor had told him that. Its size and lighting made it the perfect studio for him, but he worried his workspace was a little too bourgeois for his artist friends that rarely made it further north than the UIC campus. He had dragged them away from Sally's birthday party to impress them, but half-expected to be called a phony because he had moved out to a suburb.

He heard his wife's maniacal cackle from downstairs as she played Sorry with Trudy and Nancy's kids.

"Wow, what's going on down there?" Amanda asked as she jumped up on Wes's backed stool in front of his empty easel.

Wes turned on one of his work lights even though the track lighting overhead was on. "Sally's fulfilling her duties as drunken hostess. I've never seen her like this. Well, actually, I always see her like this whenever Trudy and Nancy come to one of our parties. The three of them always get so drunk. Which is fine because everyone just crashes in the spare bedrooms. But one of the kids is a bed-wetter."

"I love your set up, man." Amanda was a sprite of a woman with electric blue eyes and wire hair, wearing a pair of men's slacks that made her look broad in the hips, and a black t-shirt. She was the kind of woman Wes thought he would end up with. An artist.

Wes watched Juan and Saul wander through the studio, positioning themselves and looking to see how they would arrange it. *They wouldn't change anything. It's perfect.*

Juan, with the grooming of a car salesman, but in a worn flannel shirt, sat on the flat file and ran his hands along the top. "No wonder you get so much work done here."

Saul, chubby with an overlong T-shirt on and a pack of camels in his front pocket, put his hand to his whiskered chin. "I feel like I should take my shoes off to walk on dis floor. Look at dis furniture. It's friggin' cool. Where did you get it?"

Wes looked at him. He studied all three of his friends. They looked like artists while he knew he had the Mayberry deputy look. Even in high school he had dressed like a suburbanite. The thing was more and more he felt like one. Which he liked, but he was afraid his art would suffer. Because he was not suffering the way these three had to. Amanda lived in an apartment for the last six years without a shower. Juan was so far in debt; he could never get out. Saul was sure that the cleaning solvents were ruining his health, but really it was the two main tools of his art doing it- camel straights and marijuana cigarettes laced with heroin.

Amanda hefted the corner of the easel. "It's beautiful. All of it."

Juan began pushing Wes' roller bench around like a shopping cart. "Guys, this is too sweet."

Saul moved some paintings without looking at them. "Come check out his Taboret," he said. "It's like the friggin' Taj Mahal. Look at dese deep drawers." Juan opened each drawer.

Wes wanted to slap his hand away. He wanted to roll away this cart with its attached easel that he had never used away from these three artists. They weren't drooling over his creative space. Just furniture Sally had insisted on making for him.

Juan sat down at the desk with its top that could be tilted up like a drafting table. "They are like damn pieces of art. Where in the hell did you get them?"

"Sally built them."

"Do you think Sally would be interested in building me a desk like this?"

"Would she build like five of these easels? I can think of five people that would want one." Amanda caressed the easel.

"Make that six," Juan said. "If your wife will give me a deal."

"This is my studio," was all Wes could say.

"And you should be proud," Amanda replied. "Of your wife. I wish I had somebody bankrolling me."

Wes turned his work lights off. "I sell a lot of paintings."

"Oh yeah, I like dat set up, too," Saul said. "Sell dem right in Sally's shop. She brings in the big spenders with the furniture and you pull a couple of more bucks out of dem."

"That-" Wes stopped. "Let's just go back downstairs before the lesbians drink all the liquor."

Sally was still playing Sorry with Charley and Tad when Wes walked into the kitchen. Phyllis was asleep on her lap. Without looking up from the game, she told Wes, "This is the last game before they go to bed."

"Great. How are they getting home, Sally?"

"They are home. We're adopting them."

Wes flung his arms out. "Who is going to take care of them? Make breakfast for them in the morning?"

"I am."

"You? Sally it's 10:30 at night, you're playing Sorry with a nine-year-old and a seven-year-old, and your markers are four shot glasses of screaming orgasms."

"It's my birthday."

"Who is getting up with them in the morning?"

"My thirty-third birthday."

"Who's going to make them breakfast?"

"Fuck off, Wes."

"Fine. I'll go make the spare bed for Nancy and Judy and find some sleeping bags. You finish your 'talk like a sailor' lesson to the children."

Wes looked at Phyllis nestled in his wife's arms.

"What?

He couldn't tell her that even though Tad was sending her drink back to start with his Sorry card, Sally looked like she'd be a wonderful mom. "Be a good mom and have the kids go the bathroom and brush their teeth before you start puking."

Chapter 8 Always call Uncle Ralph on your birthday

U p in his bedroom, Wes saw the TV on, and an arm draped over the recliner as it faced the TV. He went and sat on the arm of the chair.

"Let's make love," the occupant of the chair said.

Wes looked down. "Not funny, Nancy. Where's my wife?"

"In the toilet, yaking her guts out. I think she's *in* the actual toilet. You should go hold her head up while she urps up her toenails."

Wes shook his head. "If I see her blow biscuits, then I'm going to scream cookies."

"It was a pretty mellow party. I can't believe she got this drunk. She spent most of the night playing board games with my kids."

"Where are your kids?"

"Helping Trudy find her bra in the front yard. Sally is so good with those kids. She's thirty-three, Wes. Do you think she wants kids?"

"Not at this moment. I don't think she would even want to try." Wes went to the master bathroom and peeked in on her. "Do you need something, Sal?"

"Uguh. Shut up. I'm going to call Ralph."

Wes walked back and sat down on the bed. He looked at the big, redheaded lesbian sitting in his recliner. Because he was an artist and diminutive, he got enough gay jokes made about himself to not judge by looks but wondered how Nancy and her ex-husband had three kids before noticing she was gay. The divorce had been rough on the children, but then Trudy came into the picture. She was a great Mom to them. Except for Sally's birthday parties. "Nancy?"

"You're wondering when I'm going to get the hell out of your bedroom, right?"

"No. Well, yeah, but I was also wondering if you know why Sally and I don't try to have kids."

"I assume it's because she has puke breath. Plus, I'm right here."

Wes smiled. "Seriously though. She really believes we will break up before our tenth anniversary and I think it's because we never had kids. But she's the one that can't make up her mind. We can have a child if she wants one."

"That doesn't help her at all."

"Sure, it does. It gives her total freedom."

Nancy shook her head. "Does Sally ever ask you if you want to go out to dinner?"

"Sure."

"Does she ever suggest where?"

"She tells me to decide."

"And where do you say you want to go."

"I tell her, 'Whatever.' I don't care normally."

"And what does Sally do?"

"She gets mad at me. Says she wants me to want to take her-—oh." Wes unbuttoned his shirt to expose his T-shirt. "Yeah, but. I have brought up having kids with her and she says she doesn't know if she wants them."

"And let me guess," Nancy said swilling her Jack and Coke. "She is so intimidated by having a baby, you guys rarely have sex."

Wes shrugged her shoulders. "Not as much as we used to."

"Have you ever thought maybe you are to blame for her, ah, non-desire?"

"Hell, yes. Even though she reassures me. Actually, because she reassures me. Which, it's not my fault. You let a guy go to the beach only one or two times a year and he won't have a lot of time to practice his swimming."

"Once or twice a year?" Trudy furrowed her brow. "Once or twice? A year?"

"That's not true," Sally whispered from the doorway of the bathroom. "I get drunk and puke at least four times a year." Sally swaggered to the bed, flapping her hands in an effort to not fall and then collapsed.

"It's my birthday and there's another woman in our bedroom, Wes." She spoke at the ceiling. "I've heard of people giving gifts they really want themselves, but this is ridiculous."

"I was exaggerating before about once or twice a year." Wes looked at Nancy for a moment with a red face. "By a lot. I can take care of her now, so you can get out of my bedroom. I can't even make one woman happy in bed. Why would I try two?"

"Ah that's sweet, honey. I heard you guys before." She looked at Nancy. "We do the deed a lot more than twice a year." Then she worked her gaze over to Wes. "Let's make some babies. I'm thirty-three now, so if I'm going to start shooting them out, we better start now."

"Shooting them out?"

Nancy jumped to her feet. "Let me get out of here before anybody shoots anything out. I was just here to make sure you didn't drown in your own sneeze cheese." Nancy kissed Sally's head. "Happy birthday, Babe."

Wes sat down on the bed and watched Nancy shut the door.

"Sally. I-"

Nancy swung the door back open. "Can I put rubber sheets on the couch for Tad or will you guys be using them?"

Sally's snore gave the answer.

WES AWOKE TO FIND SALLY staring at him, her breath immediately backing him up. "You all right, Sally?"

She reached out and touched his cheek. "I was so proud of you when we got married. I thought you were going to do everything you dreamed of doing. It made me spend the first year of our marriage trying to figure out how to keep us from breaking up."

Wes stared into her eyes. "No, you didn't. You spent it worrying about how your dad was going to live by himself."

"That too. I guess I was pretty hard to live with then."

Wes kissed her hand. "Then?"

"Okay, I'm still not that easy to live with."

"Neither am I. I don't always take the time to be a proper husband."

Sally smiled. "Am I hearing Wes Story admitting he is not perfect?"

Wes closed his eyes to get away from her gaze. "Is the way I am why you want to be divorced?"

"I don't want anything, Wes. You are the same guy I fell in love with. I'm the same crazy girl, except now I am thirty-three and afraid you are going to do everything you dreamed of doing. Then you'll be too busy being successful and we'll never have a family."

"Would you really want to start having kids?"

"Yes."

"Well, then let's.... start.... talking about doing that."

She turned onto her back. "Wes, with you leaving me in two months; it would be selfish to try."

Chapter 9 I can't deny the fact that you get me.

Instead of waiting for Jan Hutchinson in the waiting area, Wes wandered around her gallery. Besides owning the gallery putting on a whole show of Wes's work, Jan also acted as his agent and had big news for him.

He was early and Jan was on the phone. *I am not pacing,* he reassured himself as he paced. *I just liked to see my art in public.* He paced over to his section and in front of one of his paintings was a woman, black, in her early twenties, with straight, shoulder-length hair. Because she was in a black, sleeveless blouse and a black business skirt, Wes accurately took her for a new employee of the gallery.

Wes walked up and stood beside her, but she just stared at his painting, with her index finger on her mouth. "What?" Wes had to ask. "Is there a problem?"

"No," she said, her voice clear and warm. "Not at all. I was just studying this playground scene. You can tell the kids here have been playing all day at this park. Look at their dirty feet and hands and the smudges on their face."

Wes sighed. "Yes, and with the old-fashioned merry-go-round and metal slide, you are going to say it's very Norman Rockwellian. And that the painting is too nostalgic."

"No, Not at all. Look how dark the sky is. And the leaves on the trees have turned and show it's quite windy, but the kids are in summer clothes." She stepped forward. "Then do you see how this road divides the picture. Across the street is a whole other scene with a brood of kids around the dinner table with their parents. I mean it may look cutesy at first glance, but it's actually a somber painting."

"Yes," Wes said. "I can't believe it. Someone actually sees a scene as I do."

"Well, the kids are on a playground. No one cares that they are there at suppertime and its nostalgic look suggests this little scenario is nothing new. That's my interpretation anyway. I'm sure everyone understands it better than I do.

Wes grabbed her arm. "No, no they don't. They never see any of my paintings for what they are."

She peered at his signature. "You're Wes Story?"

"Yes. You work here?"

"Part-time. I'm an artist, too."

"It is an absolute pleasure to meet you-"

"Mercedes," Jan said from behind them. "Wes, if you're done gushing over my new employee, I've got some big news." Jan put her hands out as if she had just said Taadaa! or was flashing in a trench coat. She smiled, then, "I have someone that wants you to paint another mural. I guess word got out on how impressed Jewel-Osco was on theirs."

Wes did a fist pump.

"For 85,000 dollars."

Wes did many fist pumps while jumping in the air.

"In Minneapolis."

"Eh?" Wes threw his hand on his hips. "No. A mural takes weeks. Months even."

"Yeah, that's why they're going to pay you all that money. You can't pass this up, Wes. You know that. Two big murals in two different cities. This thing I got you is huge."

Wes clasped his hands behind his head. He grimaced at the thought of telling Sally. "You're right. I can't pass it up. I'll need a crew. Amanda, Saul, Juan. But I'll need more people."

"How about me?" Mercedes said, giving her own taadaa move.

Jan looked at her. "Hmm. Well, it's okay with me. I can spare you for a few weeks for my best client. If he wants you. Wes doesn't even know your work."

"She can come."

"Without even seeing her portfolio, Wes?"

Wes looked at his painting. The one Mercedes had understood when no one else, including Sally had. "Nope. She's in." Then he took his first good look at Mercedes and was struck by her big dark eyes and wide, serene smile. Next, he took in her thin body that let the fabric of her clothes state "Yes, I'm professional," except for the fun parts of her body insisting the fabric whoop "Wahoo!"

Oh, Sally is going to kill me.

Chapter 10 You'll never guess what happened to you

Wes came in through the front of Sally's furniture shop. Trudy was in the office behind the counter doing paperwork and Tad was standing on a stool, manning the cash register for the empty shop.

"Hey, Tad." Wes went to tussle his hair, but then did the more manly action of punching the boy in the shoulder. "This guy have a worker's permit, Trudy? I suspect he might be too young to work here."

"He sold one of your paintings this morning."

"Carry on then." Wes went through to the workshop. To the left of him, Nancy was in the paint booth. In spite of the painting area being curtained by plastic and having its own ventilation system, the whole shop smelled strongly of varnish. Sally's dad, John, was running boards through the planer. The planer went from a hum to a howl as it accepted a board and pulled the board through itself. John fed the raw board and then went to the other side to take smooth product as it came out.

Tiffany and Ellie were on sweeping detail and Sally was in the far-left corner of the shop, cutting out a pattern with a router. The router looked like Rosie the Robot on the Jetsons except for the bottom where the bit cut into the wood and Sally was holding onto the handles on either side of the tool like she was trying to drown Michael Phelps.

Everyone was wearing work boots, jeans, and safety glasses. Their typical uniform while Wes always seemed to be coming from the

35

gallery where he wore slacks and hush puppies. Of course, the closest thing he had to work boots was his rubber overshoes.

"Hi, Mr. Story," the girls giggled in unison.

John nodded to him.

For a reason Wes couldn't figure out, Nancy grabbed her left boob and shook it at him.

"What's the matter?" Sally yelled over the router. "You don't ever come visit me unless it's bad news."

Wes switched his smile on like a neon sign for a strip club. "No, good news."

"Huh?"

"Nothing bad."

Sally turned the router off. "Nothing too bad?"

Wes waited to speak because John was also done on his machine, but before the planer whined completely down, John started the table saw that hummed quieter until Wes opened his mouth to talk. As John ran a board through, the saw let out a high pitch whine.

Wes yelled, "It's always so crazy when I'm here. Is it always like this?"

At this moment, the table saw kicked back a board and sent it sailing into the overhead door where it crashed with a large bang. "What crazy?" Sally yelled back.

"Get ready to congratulate me. I have a new commission. For a mural." John turned the saw off to retrieve his board. Wes, still yelling, had his last words echo. "In Minneapolis."

"Damn it, Wes." Her words echoed in the shop, too. The machines now completely silent.

Sally turned and walked toward the storeroom. "Who is she?"

Wes followed her. "Who is who?"

"Who are you cheating on me with? I find it a little convenient that you need to disappear for a large stretch of time."

"This is my career. This is life."

"Look at my dad. He was never away from home for more than a day, or we went with him. He put his family first."

"And his wife left him. He sacrificed his whole life for a nut job. Sorry John."

John nodded his head toward Sally. "It's your wife you need to worry about, son."

Sally stalked into the storeroom with Wes following. *My employees will have to remain motionless to hear this now.* Sally thought. *Not a problem for them.* "How could you say that about my dad?"

"I don't think he'd do it the same if he had to do it over again."

"I wanted to be a stewardess, but I chose a career that kept me close to you."

Wes glanced around, regretting he had walked into a room with some good head-knocking two by fours. "You are too tall to be a stewardess and you had the shop before we got married."

"A trucker then."

"Sally, please be logical. This is a big paycheck for me and for my crew and I'll be home every weekend."

"Who is she?" Sally set her black safety glasses into her hair. Sighed. "I mean who's on the crew?"

Mercedes. Juan, Amanda Saul. Saul Juan Mercedes Amanda. Alphabetical? Amanda, Juan, Mercedes, and Saul. "You know, Amanda Saul Juan. Mercedes. I'll hire some students from the University of Minnesota-"

"Who's Mercedes? I don't know a Mercedes. I don't even like foreign cars."

The intercom clicked on, and it was Tad's voice. "Aunt Sally. Come up here right now. It's an emergency."

Sally flew out of the room, to where Ellie and Nancy were standing in the doorway between the shop and store. Sally heaved herself passed them into the store and everyone followed her. Wes followed everyone else.

Trudy was standing between Tiffany and a large burly man.

"I'm getting my daughter," the burly man said, trying to lunge around Trudy and grab his daughter.

Trudy stepped into his lunge. "She doesn't want to go with you,"

"I don't want her being infiltrated by you carpet munchers. You'll turn her into one of youse." He caught Tiffany's arm with a juke and a lunge. "Let's go."

Sally grabbed her other arm. "She wants to stay here." she barked. "And you know it."

The burly guy looked over to John. "You dike-lovin' pervert. All these years I've known youse. I let her take this job 'cause I trusted you to take care of my daughter, not throw her in with a bunch of muff divers. If my daughter becomes one of them, I'll hold you responsible."

"You're going to have to let her go, Nancy," John said from the doorway.

"You agree with him don't you, John?"

"What are you going to do? She's sixteen and his daughter." John let silence settle for a moment. "Tiffany?" John asked in his cop voice. "Are you afraid your dad is going to hurt you?"

She looked at her dad. "No."

"Verbally abuse you?"

"He's going to yell at me. But no."

"Then, you are going to have to go with your dad."

"I can't believe you are going to take his fucking side," Nancy said to John.

"I'm not taking sides."

The burly guy held the door open for his daughter to walk through.

"But," John said. "Here's a piece of advice, Carl. Eventually she's going to do what she wants to do. Behavior like this will make her more rebellious and determined to defy you." John turned and went back into the shop.

Sally rushed along with the rest to watch Tiffany get into her dad's truck. She felt she had not stood up for her friends and that through her dad she had let them down. Trudy, Nancy, and Tiffany.

Without looking at Wes who stood next to her, she said, "You'll be going to Minneapolis over my dead body."

Chapter 11 S.O.S. Sally Olivia Story

Sally's work boots thudded on the tile floor; noise never heard in Jan's gallery before. She scanned the room for the enemy.

"Hello," Mercedes said from behind her as she had been dusting the pictures in the store window. "Can I help you?"

Sally looked at this girl's short skirt and form fitting sleeveless top. She stuffed her gloves a little further into her back pocket. "I sure hope not."

"Excuse me?"

"I need to talk to Jan."

"Jan's at lunch. I'm sure I can help you."

"Can you get someone else to do the mural in Minnesota? Replace Wes? Can you do that Miss High-Heel Open Toe?"

"Why would we want to do that? Mr. Story is the most talented artist Jan has."

"Listen, I'm sure she gets a commission and it's a nice little paycheck for the cronies he's taking with him-"

"We're not going for the money."

"What? Who we? Amanda, Saul, and Juan are going. And this chick named Mazda.....Ooohh. I was afraid you looked like you."

"I'm Mercedes. Now who are you?"

"Sally Story."

"Distant Cousin?"

"Wife. And you better be kidding about going with."

"No. Wes offered me the opportunity. Even though we had just met."

"Really?" Sally bit her lip. She was also biting her tongue.

"So, I can tell you, it's not about the money. I mean I am a single parent on fixed income. But this is a chance to be a part of something big. Why wouldn't you want Wes to go? I'm amazed by his work."

"I guess, maybe, the one I need to talk to is Mr. Story. Thank you, Ms.-"

"Mercedes. Just call me Mercedes."

"How exotic and sexy. It fits you, dear." Sally turned and took a few thuds towards the door but stopped and turned around. "Don't pack your lace panties yet. If I have any sway over my husband, there will be no trip to paint this mural."

Chapter 12 Jim Morrison and Pat Boone were both artists.

A t the foot of the stairs, Sally stopped for a moment. The first thing she would see as she made her way into the loft would be his leather loafers. At Lincoln Park High School, most of the boys had worn destroyed jeans and Tretorns tennis shoes, and all of the boys interested in her wore the jersey of the sport they played and trackpants. However, Sally had found herself looking around campus for Wes. He wandered the school in a sweater and his hush puppies, quietly observing everything around him.

He was a geek and her friends made fun of her crush on him. However, he was confident, and she liked that. He noticed her looking at him, strolled over in those shoes, and asked her out.

Even though he was only seventeen, he was already renting a studio apartment. It was the apartment above his parents' garage, but his art afforded him rent money and trust from his parents.

Trust enough that he easily snuck Sally up to his studio and they made love with the windows open. Or shut on cold nights. However, they did like to listen to the rain during thunderstorms. After they made love, they talked and shared everything. In the morning, she would wake up to find him in the early morning light, already painting and it was like they were still talking and sharing everything.

Sally snuck up to Wes's studio. Wes was sock footed. Loudly, to startle him, she yelled, "You used my hammer and didn't put it back." She held it out for him to see.

"I'm going to do that mural," he said.

"I'm not up here for that. I want you to stop using my tools and not putting them back."

"No. You're here to argue with me about my trip. I'm only working on what I've dedicated my life to doing, so you thought it'd be a good time to interrupt me." Wes leaned over to look at the hammer in her hand. "That's your centipede hammer. You keep it in the bathroom to squish centipedes."

"And who hammered the last centipede and put my hammer back under the sink. You need to leave it in the middle of the floor for quick access."

"You can come with me." Wes sat on the stool with his palette firmly around his thumb. "Put Trudy in charge of the shop for a few weeks and spend time with me in the twin cities."

"I can't Wes. I'm needed here. I have orders to fill that my customers expect to be handled by me. Troubles are brewing, too. Nancy and Trudy aren't talking to my dad because he didn't stand up for them. Which I think he's on edge because the anniversary of mom leaving is coming up. Tiffany came back but is in constant fear her dad is going to find out she is sneaking to work. Then, to top it off, Trudy and Nancy are having troubles with Tad, and they aren't even talking to each other."

"Sounds like who they need is Dr. Phil." Wes looked at his painting. "Maybe I need you to be with me."

"So, I can sit in a hotel room and watch TV while you work long hours? I need you here."

"You don't need me, Sally. The only thing I did for you you couldn't do for yourself is kill bugs. And now you have your centipede hammer."

"I can't believe this. I ask you to do one thing for me and you refuse." Sally paced with the hammer in her hand. "If you love me, you will call this whole mural thing off."

"You'll see, Sal. The weeks will fly by, and I will be able to afford to take you some place wonderful for our anniversary. We'll do something we've never done before."

"Like litigation." Sally pointed the hammer at him. "You are not going."

Chapter 13 Next on Lifetime

Wes put the phone down from ordering the pizzas and it began ringing again.

"You haven't called me," Sally said.

"Hi, Sal."

"It's been five days and you didn't call me once."

"You told me if I tried to call you, you would file divorce papers."

"You should have still tried. Well, how's it going up there?"

"It was another long day, and it doesn't seem like we get anything done."

"Well, what are you doing now?"

"Sitting in my hotel room with Mercedes." Wes looked over to Mercedes at the small round table, not flipping through the channels or reading the hotel literature expounding on the services all hotels have. She was not pretending to be not listening. Instead, she was watching him.

"What? Did you just do her or are you about to?"

"We're waiting for Saul to come back with paper plates."

"I'm supposed to believe that?"

"If I was doing something, wouldn't I have just said I was alone?"

"No because the person that the person is not alone with always tries to be daring by making noises because she wants the marriage to end."

"Only in movies on the Lifetime channel."

"Because they follow true life."

"Here's Saul coming through the door. Say hi to my crazy wife, Saul." He heard the line click.

Chapter 14 It's not like she's Genghis Khan

Things had gone well the second week. Amanda and Juan were back at the hotel, having decided to spend their Saturday morning watching cartoons and getting high. Saul was making a run for supplies and the college helpers he had hired had all gone back to their hometowns for the weekend.

That left Wes and Mercedes alone behind the plastic curtain surrounding the mural. With no one else in the building, Mercedes decided just to wear a sweatshirt and sweatpants. They were having a nice conversation, but Wes had to keep telling himself that the way the soft material clung to her butt and the soft, gray curves of the sweatshirt were not driving him crazy.

"This is great to be able to paint in peace and quiet. But maybe you should have gone home this weekend. Your wife seemed pretty mad the other night."

Good. Let's talk about my wife. That should get rid of my lust- - I mean give me a chance to mention I love my wife. After pizza, he had stayed up late and got caught up in watching a movie on Lifetime that showed him an emotional affair was just as bad as a physical one. He was sure he wasn't having one, but he enjoyed working with Mercedes and he had come to rely on her to help him with his mural. He also looked forward to seeing her and spending as much time with her as he could.

He finished blending a line. *You are loyal to to...Sally. Why couldn't I think of her name?* "I knew calling her crazy was going to cause problems when I said it. I still said it."

"You wanted to upset her."

"No, not really. I just thought it was the fastest way to end the argument. We were not going to make-up, so why go on with the back and forth? That's what we do. We are very different people and fight a lot. Which I guess kinds of works for us." Wes took his large brush and went over a rock one of the students had painted but had been too stingy with the paint. He wanted everything strong and textured. "Those fights don't even upset me anymore."

Mercedes had been sitting on the floor by the paints, trying to remix a color she wasn't happy with. She came back to the spot she had been working on which made her shoulder to shoulder with Wes.

"That's sad. Relationships shouldn't be like that."

"Things will go on," Wes continued. "We will get over the fight. Things will get better." Wes decided Mercedes smelled nice. It was probably why he did not and should have told her that fights were okay because Sally was the best person he knew. "Of course, then there will be another big, terrible fight."

"That's no way to live, Wes."

Wes made eye contact as she was looking at him. She turned back to the mural. "Something tells me it is the only way there is to live. I don't want anything else."

"Wes. You should be treated better. And if she won't treat you better, then you should find someone willing to."

"Mercedes, it might look like there's problems from the outside. Especially for someone as young as you." Wes worked to say the right words to defend his relationship and his wife. "But there's nothing particularly bad about Sally."

"I don't know if you really think that's true."

"Everyone has their faults. We have to accept them and work through them the best we can."

"So, are you going to call her tonight?"

"No way in hell. She hung up on me."

Chapter 15 The more things stay the same, the more things stay the same.

S ally pulled off her gloves and shut the door to muffle the sound of the jointer. She sat down at her desk and scratched at a ring of dried varnish on her desk. The old metal desk was in her office that she never used, but she pulled a scraper out of her tool belt and jutted into the ring before picking up the phone.

"Hi, honey," she sang into the phone. Then she hrmpfed.

There was a brief silence, then Wes' voice. "Hello, Sally. It's quiet. Are you actually *in* your office?"

"Why is there something you need from it? About the only thing in here though is the mop bucket."

"Thank you for that. I didn't want to compete with the sound of the band saw. Look- we're coming home today."

"We? Have you met someone away at college?"

"I am. My crew and I are coming home for the weekend. We're leaving in a couple of hours."

"And you want me to be waiting in something sexy with a home cook meal? Is that it, Wes? Is that why you're calling me?"

"You don't have to change clothes for me."

"What?"

"I just mean I've been eating takeout for the last three weeks."

"Then you must have had your fill of seeing Mercedes wearing something sexy."

"No. Not at all."

"Oh. I suppose. How could you have had your fill with her being so young?"

"Knock it off. Sally."

"Don't get angry with me. I haven't been the one away for two weeks without calling."

"You didn't call me either."

"I'm not the one that went away. I'm right where I thought I would be in communicating distance, but you moved seven hours away." Wes didn't say anything and to fill the void, Sally scraped at another dried gob on her desk. *Ketchup?* she asked herself. "Somebody's been using my own personal sanctuary without permission."

"Mercedes and I are just friends, Sal."

Sally was silent for a second. "What are we? We need to talk about that. You need to get your priorities straight here and we need to talk about our relationship and start putting it first."

"That's why I'm calling. We need to talk tonight."

"Not tonight. I have volleyball." Sally heard a thumping sound. "What was that?"

"Me hitting myself in the head with the phone."

"I'm sorry, but you're the one that left me here all alone."

"Did you want to support me for the rest of our lives?"

"Yes. That's exactly what I want to happen. I want things to stay the same."

"Regardless of what I want." He hung up the phone.

Chapter 15 On the bubble

Sally propped herself up in the doorframe of the store.

Trudy looked up from the paperwork she was doing at the counter. "What's up boss?"

"Someone's been eating in my office."

"You have an office?"

"Yes." Sally put her hand on her hip. "You know, the room with the bathroom supplies?"

"Oh, that's me. Sorry, Boss."

"Knock it off." Sally sat down in the chair where Phyllis usually sat after school and colored. "There's no reason to call me the B word. I just want to know why you haven't been eating lunch with the rest of us. What the hell is going on with you and Nancy?"

"She expects me to be a parent- to be loving and supportive and pay for braces."

"The witch."

"That's not the problem. It's that when I try to discipline the children, she thinks I'm being mean and uncaring because I'm not their real mom. Tad is getting into a lot of trouble and needs to be reigned in."

"Tad's always been, ah, high strung."

"Naughty. That's the word you wanted to say. But I don't blame him. He's been having a lot of trouble with what other kids say about his mom and me. He gets picked on and gets into a fight because people call us names. It's why I think gays shouldn't be allowed to adopt. I wouldn't want to subject children to the ridicule and teasing from other kids. I went through the same thing with my parents being drunks in a small town. Like Tad, I was angry and out of control. That's why I want to give him consequences. That's what I needed."

Sally adjusted in her seat. "His problem might run a little deeper. I remember hearing about sex and then realizing my parent's bumped uglies. Part of me still pretends it didn't happen between my mommy and daddy. Do you remember the first time you thought of your parents doing it?"

"Thanks to you, I'm picturing how I didn't have to conjure it up because lots of time they were so drunk they forgot to shut their bedroom door."

"That's frightening."

"Psychosis inducing."

"Now try to picture your mom having sex with another woman."

Sally shuttered.

Nancy shuddered, too. "Stop it, Sally. Those kids are loved and taken care of. Yet, I still feel guilt that my sex life makes it harder on those kids. And now I feel like I'm abandoning them. I'm pretty much staying at my mom's trailer full time and spend time at home only for the kids. But we can't just stay together for them."

"What else would keep people together?"

"Ah, love, Sally. I want a relationship that is successful."

"And success is?" Sally pulled a small level out of her tool belt and tested how level the counter between them sat.

"Not falling out of love and hating each other. Not breaking up."

Sally reached down with a wooden shimmy from her tool belt and jammed it under a leg. "Then your only successful relationship is the one that kills you."

"Nancy is always telling me I've never had a lasting relationship before."

"Well, no shit. If you had one that lasted, you wouldn't have been available for Nancy. Maybe instead of telling you what you think, she should be dealing with her own feelings." Sally tapped the desk, gave the shim a kick and then holstered her level. "God, she is so pig-headed."

"I know, but don't be mad at her. Things may still work out. Those kids have already been through so much."

Sally looked down at her ring. "You're lucky. You two have kids that will force you to work things out. I had to come up with a plan."

Chapter 16 The bony feet of love

Wes opened the door to the empty house to have Bobvila jump up and lick his face. "Bobs, I missed you too."

The dog jumped down and came back with his leash in his mouth while making an urgent whining sound. Wes let the dog lead him through the back of the house and opened the door for him. The sun had just gone down, and Wes smelled the wet grass and heard the crickets. As his eyes adjusted to the darkness of the backyard, he noticed one of the abundant rabbits twenty feet in front of him. For his constant argument that since the dog was Sally's, she should take Bobvila out to do his business, Wes secretly coveted the last potty break of the night. As a bachelor, he had lived in Pilsen and even though his apartment/studio had looked onto a quiet garden area, it wasn't even close to being as peaceful and dark as his own backyard. Plus, he never would have risked being outside in Pilsen after dusk.

I am not a city guy, he thought to himself, picturing Mercedes as a part of a Chicago scene. Then he pictured the hotel room he had stayed in for the last three weeks. *I am not a traveler either*. His next thought he ignored because it was, *I am middleclass*.

Instead, he stepped out onto the grass that hadn't been mowed in three weeks and took in a new smell from the bottom of his shoe. "Crap," he said. And it indeed was. He took a step forward and discovered he was in a crap landmine field. "Bobs. Bobs, let's go." But Bobvila was in the back corner marking his territory.

Wes scraped his shoes off on the side of the steps as he went up on the deck and tried to remember that he was happy to be home. It was after all his deck, his planked platform allowing him to be in his backyard without touching the ground. Well, he didn't quite know the purpose of having a deck, but he knew he liked having one and right now it was a safe ship on the crap sea of his lawn.

The miasmic smell from the bottom of his shoe made him take his shoes off on the far end of the deck and walked to the patio door. "Bobs," he yelled. "Now." The dog immediately ran to the door and scratched on the glass impatiently before Wes got it open.

Wes had Bobvila in a headlock as he tried to wipe any poop off his paws with a paper towel when Sally appeared in the kitchen.

"Please don't wrestle with a dirty animal in my kitchen."

"I am trying to wipe his feet off."

"I'm talking to the dog."

"With all that dog mess in the backyard, his feet are disgusting."

"That's why I take him out with a leash. I know the clear spots. Didn't he give you his leash?"

"No. Are you waiting for the dog to bring you a shovel and a bucket before you go on poop patrol?"

"I was waiting for you to mow the lawn."

Wes sighed. Not exactly, the way he wanted to start the reconciliation. Sally's next comment wasn't a good start either.

"We should have had kids."

"We can have a kid. I wanted you to be ready."

"And I wanted you to want children with me so bad that you hounded me for it."

Wes looked at her. He cocked an eyebrow. "Okay. Part of your wifely duties is to give me someone to carry on my name. So, let's get cracking."

"Thank you for that. But it's too late."

"It's only a little after ten. Take a shower and that will wake you up."

"No. Now it's too late with you leaving me."

"Will you stop saying that?"

"Make me."

"Let's not be childish."

"No, lets. Be so upset at the thought of losing me that you do something foolish. To make me believe we are going to be together forever. Convince me I'm wrong."

"I can't predict the future."

"Wrong answer."

"Why do you always say we're going to break up if you don't want to break up? If it's something you believe, well maybe you know better than I do. Is it something you feel in your gut or are you saying it just to win an argument?"

"I'm not trying to win anything."

"Are you saying this stuff just to goad me?"

"Yes."

"Because this is serious. We need to be honest."

"I said, 'yes.' I want you to fight for me."

"I fight with you. Isn't that the same thing?"

"You're not funny."

"I was being serious. I truly don't understand what you want from me."

"I saw my parents drift apart. My mom developed her own set of friends and activities to replace Dad and he did nothing to win her back. He just let her leave."

"I'm sorry, Sally."

"And I'll do the same thing if you're not careful. I'm the same as her. I had the choice tonight of playing volleyball and saving our marriage and look what I chose."

"I understand why you did that."

"And you're just like him."

"You're saying your six-three, retired police officer and part-time carpenter father and your five foot seven, handsome, but scrawny artist husband are similar?"

"Yes. You both go to your work area and hide out."

Wes took off his socks. With being in them all day and having walked across the deck in them, he couldn't stand having them on anymore. He figured she was wrong. He wanted to ask her if a lawyer going off to court was hiding out. If a dentist was hiding out in his office. *Yes, your dad was hiding from your mom. However, painting is my vocation. I am not hiding. I'm living life on my own terms.*

"Can I take your bony white feet as a sign you want to be here and fight for me?"

"Definitely." Saying that stirred his emotions. Made it true. It rose up in him that he wanted to make his wife happy. This mixed in with lust from not being with his wife for three weeks. He went to her and kissed her. Then folded in was his guilt from some of his lust coming from working next to Mercedes for those three weeks. His concoction of feelings was slathered in the knowledge they had not really talked things through. He pulled at her shorts, brushing aside his conflicted feelings. He felt like a man.

AFTER MAKING LOVE ON the kitchen table and then the rug in front of the empty fireplace, they laid together with Sally's long leg draped over him as he lay on his back.

"Can we just keep our old life?" Sally asked him.

"Our old life where I was depressed and emasculated because I wasn't paying any of the bills and you felt taken advantage of until you wanted to rip out my spleen?"

"We'll just rewind to a few weeks before that happens. I'll be happier this time because I'll know what I could lose. Let someone else finish the mural and cancel your shows you have coming up in New York."

"When I am so close to becoming known nationally? So close to what I always wanted?"

"Why is that what you want?"

"That's a stupid question."

"Is it?"

"So's that one."

Sally rolled away from him and grabbed her clothes. Standing up, she clutched her clothes to curtain her chest and gut that in their ten years had gone from almost belly ring flat to flabby. She tried to never be naked around him, but he liked her the way she was. She had held up better than some women her age and he liked the trade-off of being able to go out with her for a bag of White Castle sliders and not have her get worked up over the calories. Still, angry and naked was not a good look for his wife.

"Just answer my stupid question. Why is becoming famous what you want? To be rich?"

"You know I don't care about that. I just want people to experience my work. I think I have a message. That's why I want it."

"Aren't people experiencing your paintings now? What would be the difference if you were famous?"

"More would see it."

"Really? Is that right, Wes? Is that true?"

"I want to do something for humanity."

"And I want you to want to do something for me."

Their slowly rising voices stopped.

"You want me to go back to being a nobody artist, unknown except for a few paintings I sell out of your shop."

"Yes. See? Simple."

"So, I give up everything I worked for and what about you?"

"I keep on loving you."

"That just doesn't seem like a fair trade-off."

"Goddamn you."

Wes was laying with his head propped up on his arm and a couch pillow in front of his lap. "Come on, Sally." He felt awkward, so he sat up and found himself crotch level looking up at Sally. He pushed himself back and sat his bare butt on the cold bricks of the fireplace's hearth. "What do I get for giving up all my dreams?"

"Now that's a stupid question," she said and danced herself between the couch and coffee table. He heard her feet on the steps and thought he should follow her. At the same time, he figured he would just hurt the situation more, like jamming a stick into the spokes of his own wheelchair.

Chapter 17 If you leave, you're kicked out

Wes unburied himself from unconsciousness and then from the couch cushions. He patted the floor under the couch for his glasses until he finally let himself just slip to the floor so he could search for his glasses like a mole.

With his glasses on, he looked eyelevel at the clock on the DVD player. 1:56 pm. *Two in the afternoon?* he thought. *No, wait. We don't know how to set that thing.* He looked at his wristwatch on the coffee table. It was 10:00.

He jumped up as if that would help him with the fact, he was four hours late to begin his morning painting. He ran upstairs and found mounds of dirty clothes in their bedroom, but Sally gone. *I didn't even hear her clod hopping around for work. Damn it.*

I've never gotten up later than Sally. Not even sick.

He scooped her clothes off the floor, but then threw them down. He wanted to storm out of the room but couldn't. His need for order forced him to put away a basket of her clean clothes and strip-mine the terrain of dirty clothes into the empty basket. He tamped the clothes down with his foot to fit more in, threw her sport bras on top, and stomped on them to stomp on them. He ground his heel into her jeans with the underwear still in them. *White, cotton panties that need to be damn Separated.*

In retaliation, the clothes tried to jump to freedom as he carried two baskets of them to the basement. A couple of socks evacuated on the steps. A T-shirt grabbed hold of the basement doorknob. They shouldn't have stranded themselves. For when Wes dropped the basket waist-high to the basement floor, most of the clothes tumbled out like kids abandoning a toboggan after a big crash into the neighbor's garage.

He angrily separated her colors from whites and jeans from undies and ran a load of her wash. It was only after he hauled down a third basket of clothes that he saw the note on the table.

Wes-

Below is the address of the loft I rented for you and the check is for the first month's rent. I have paid the security deposit already. I want you to go live there because I am tired of fighting all the time. I picked out a place you can live and work in. In the end, I couldn't take your painting away from you. Please note the rental is too small to have friends over.

Sally

On the floor were several boxes. Because Sally had not bothered to close them up or really even pack them carefully, he saw one of them had his painting supplies and toiletries.

He sat down at their kitchen table for the second time in his life.

Then he let the dog out, picked up doggy mines, and put her clothes in the dryer. With ever-increasing anger, he did a second and third load of her clothes, folded them fresh out of the dryer, and then tore off to meet his new landlord.

When he couldn't put it off any longer.

Chapter 18 A clown painting of me and you

W es listened, his phone tight to his ear to hear Sally's every word. "I just feel this is the best for us and for the future of our marriage. I want us to start communicating honestly. I know I have some issues with my parents, but you have your issues too. I guess- this is hard. I guess I have been avoiding my feelings for too long. Before I met you even. What we need to do now is start being open and start a real dialogue."

There was a click. "If you would like to save this message as new, press 1," the concatenated voice of his voice mail said. "If you would like to delete this message-" Wes pressed two. "You have no new messages."

Wes fastened the phone back onto his belt holder and watched as Jan shut the door to her office and walked toward him. She tugged the lapels of her blazer across her chest. Jan, a stout woman with hair past her shoulders looked to Wes like a stay-at-home mom. However, she strode across the large room with the confidence of a businessperson.

"Wes, thanks for meeting me now." Her voice was that of a schmoozer, but a sincere schmoozer.

"Whatever you need, Jan," he replied with his own chatter voice. "The truth is I needed a break from painting." This was a lie. He had spent his weekend of complete freedom and solace to paint un-interrupted watching infomercials and talk shows. He only had an hour of painting in before coming because he tried to sketch Dr. Oz as a guest on the Dr Phil show. Except instead of Dr Phil, it was Bob Newhart in a plaid leisure suit.

"I just like scheduling meetings over the lunch hour to have an artist here at our busiest time. It sells paintings. Walk with me." Jan resumed her pace. "So, are you all set to fill this gallery?" she called over her shoulder.

"I have a couple ready."

In a simple turn, Jan was nose to nose with him. "What? I need to have them all ready, Wes. I expect you to be able to fill this gallery twice. Twice-"

"Jan, I'm kidding. I have enough for three shows."

"Don't do that to me okay? You'd be surprised at the number of artists I get that are on their own schedules. They don't realize things not going smoothly is money out of my pocket."

"I'm ready, Jan."

"And it's not because of the money. I can't help artists if I'm closed."

"Actually, you closing would probably help save my marriage."

Jan pressed her nose into his and took his arm. "I cannot deal with a divorce right now."

"I'm kidding, Jan. Just kidding."

"You don't joke, Wes."

"Well, I thought I'd give it a try."

"See? That's not funny." They walked over to where Wes' paintings were a part of a group exhibit. They passed Mercedes who touched his arm and gave him a warm hello.

A warm hello that made him want to talk to her and tell her all that had happened in the few days since he had last seen her. He knew too, that to want to tell her was bad.

"When are you going to be done using Mercedes, Wes?"

"I- hey- what?"

"When are you going to be done with the mural? I need her here at the gallery. And quite frankly Michael needs her too."

"Michael? Is that her boyfriend?"

"Her son. He must have come up in conversations. You've worked closely with her for the last three weeks."

Wes was sure he had just turned green and thought maybe his knees had buckled because he couldn't feel them. He still seemed to be standing though. The first thing he realized was he hadn't stopped talking about himself to find out about her. Then he asked himself, *Why do I feel like I just dodge a bullet...especially since I wasn't even on the firing range thingy.*

"You know that's why she works here right?" Jan asked. "She can't support herself and little Michael as an artist."

"Then why did she go with me to do the mural?"

Jan looked at him with a crooked eyebrow. "Because she *is* an artist, Wes. It is actually being paid to paint and Michael's father can swing taking him. Normally, you're such a good listener. It's what makes you a good businessman. I really don't understand how you didn't acquire any of this information. Especially since she has a crush on you."

Wes turned his body so he was facing the rest of the gallery and Mercedes. He saw her at the front counter, realized how obvious he was being, and pivoted back to his original position. "She only works here twenty-five hours a week?"

"Twenty-seven."

"I still don't know how you know that much about her in twenty-seven hours a week."

Jan tugged him into motion again. "I have to be able to glean things like that to be successful." Jan touched one of the three patrons on the arm. "There are more landscapes down and to the left. Let me know if you need anything ma'am. I'm Jan Hutchinson, the owner of the gallery."

"Oh, thank you," the elderly patron said.

"Plus, she's kinda a blabbermouth. Still, I can find out a lot about a person just by looking at them. Take you for example. My normally fastidious Wes has scraped his knuckles, which suggest carrying boxes.

I couple that with those streaks on your shirt, which comes from a crappy wash machine and a powder detergent from a vending machine. You have changed residences. You have about four days growth of beard which suggests you were expecting sex when you got home from the twin cities, but after that you knew you weren't getting any. I say Sally kicked you out the morning after you got back.

"She get you an apartment in Pilsen?"

"Yeah."

Jan shook her head. "The fact you have been painting and that you walked here show that. See? I know everything."

Wes decided to stump her. "Then why did Sally kick me out?"

"Well, because she loves you." Jan answered without missing a beat.

"That does sound like Sally."

"It's true. You guys have been married for ten years and don't have kids. It also seems to her that you left for Minneapolis too easily and were doing fine without her. She is questioning her value as a woman. I went through the same thing in my 30's. We women have come a long way. Sometimes though, we still feel June Cleaver emotions."

"Oh."

"Now couple that with the fact you just spent three weeks with a woman that has the hots for you, and you get a woman desperate for changes. Sounds about right, doesn't it?"

"I have no clue what's going on with Sally," he said too loudly.

"I am not surprised." Jan went down to a whisper. "You do see that Mercedes has a thing for you?

Wes nodded.

"No, you really don't. You might even think you know, but you don't. Well, she does, Wes. She sees an artist, a kindred spirit. But she also sees a commission to do an expensive mural, that you are going to have your own show, and how you are on the cusp of having your work shown nationally. To be straight forward, she's infatuated with you because you can provide for her."

"Good. At least someone finally does. That'd be a new sensation. To feel like a man."

"I'd ask you if you were joking, but you're not." She touched his arm and nodded to a lady in her early fifties standing in front of one of his paintings. "She was in here last week over lunch with her mother looking at your clown painting."

"Clown painting? I don't have a clown painting."

"The one with the clown in it?"

"You mean Desecration of a Childhood."

"She thinks it's cute."

His painting was of a small boy hiding behind his mother's apron as the clown hired for his backyard birthday party coaxes him to take a balloon animal. Behind the clown a few, scattered children eat birthday cake at a picnic table. The sky is cloudless, and the grass is lush.

Wes snapped to it. "Do you like my painting, ma'am?"

"Well, yes, I do. You painted this? You really tried to capture the innocence and peace of an earlier time, didn't you?"

"You have obviously never had a clown come to your birthday party, lady." Wes remembered the clown for his seventh birthday and how few kids showed up for his tenth. He thought it was obvious how he had painted the mother's apron strings as tendrils wrapping ever tighter around the small boy.

"Wes," Jan said.

"I mean yes. Children today see murders on TV and movies with special effects. They aren't entertained or scared by clowns anymore." Wes stood on the back of his heels. "Not like in the good old days." *Lucky kids.*

"So, I'm right?"

"Well...Did you happen to notice my use of green and purple, and then the muted red of the mother's apron?"

"Yes. They make me think of innocence. Maybe I got it wrong though. I'm not an expert."

"Ma'am. A work of art is not complete until someone looks at it. You complete my painting. So, you have to go with the initial impact the painting has on you. If it doesn't wow you, then move on. But if it stirs something in your soul, then you need to get it and it will only grow in depth for you." Wes believed what he was saying strongly. It was why he couldn't change his style, even though nobody seemed to get it and took his melancholy pictures for nostalgia. Emotion ran so strong in his paintings (what was scarier or more beautiful than reality) that sometimes they appeared to be innocuous.

Jan smiled at the impact Wes was having on the patron.

"Like a marriage," the lady suggested.

Wes looked at his painting. He remembered working on it and not thinking about anything else, but what was going on in it. "Except the painting won't cause you to move into a studio apartment."

Chapter 19 Talk from Uranus

Trudy sat on a stool reading *Men Are from Mars, Women are from Venus* and tried to decide which planet she was from. A relationship is a relationship she figured, but the book was not addressing the problems she was having with Nancy. When she looked up, Sally was in front of her.

"Hiya, Boss."

"You know, you could be dusting or doing inventory."

"Done. So is the payroll, the truck order, our quarterly taxes, and the thank you notes to our recent customers."

"You do all that? Well, watch the store, I have to go out."

"I'm in charge of the store. It's what you hired me to do. But it's not like you to leave during the day."

"Wes is coming to pick up all of his paintings."

"Shouldn't you be here for that?"

"If you don't want to deal with him, I can send Nancy up." Trudy pointed to the book and shook her head. "I can send my dad then?"

"I don't think he likes Nancy and me anymore. Do you think he has a problem with us because of what Tiffany's dad said?"

"I don't know. Do you have a problem with my father?"

"No. Not at all. He is polite, but so reserved around us."

"I think my dad has a problem interacting with women in general."

"He is very friendly with Ellie and Tiffany."

"They're kids or at least he sees them as kids. This means he doesn't consider either one as a possible partner and therefore is not afraid of them."

"You think he's sees us as possible partners?"

"My dad is as strait-laced as they come. But men's instincts are still at the caveman level."

"I think you should be here when Wes gets here. You should talk to him."

"And I think *you* should."

Trudy slid off the stool. "Well, I guess I misjudged who I am working for. First, you kick Wes out of the house and now you won't even let him keep his paintings in your store. What kind of jerk are you?"

"He's just taking his pictures to the gallery. For. His. Opening."

Trudy sat back down. "Sorry, Babe. I really just want the two of you to work things out. Are you mad?"

"Yes."

"Am I fired?"

"Probably."

"Do you still love me?"

"Always." Sally re-slung her purse over her shoulder and slid out the door before Wes arrived. Still, she had to pop her head back in. "You're not going to fill Wes with advice on how to work things out with me, are you?"

"I am."

"What if I fire you?"

"Then right after I talk to Wes, I will go look for a new job."

"Thanks Trudy."

Chapter 20 Catch-22

When Wes tucked himself into the store, Trudy placed her book upside down and said, "Well."

"Ah, hi Trudy. Sally around?"

"No, she left because she misses you too much."

"Of course, she did." Wes picked one of his pictures off the wall. Then he set it down. "Listen, I wanted to ask you how Sally is doing."

"She's doing all those things people should do when they are going through a rough time- staying active, meditating, hanging out with lesbians, but- I wanted to tell you before you heard any rumors- she has also been hanging out with one of the guys on her volleyball team. She's not close to doing anything stupid, I don't think, but does hang out with him to kill time."

"Is he a lesbian as well?"

"I can't always hang out with her. I got responsibilities at home."

"She's really meditating? My meat and potatoes wife?"

"She misses you. She'd never admit it, but she's lonely without you."

"That's probably why she's doing all that meditating. With that other guy."

"You haven't made much of an attempt to win her back."

"She kicked me out. Does she sit cross-legged and hum?"

"Wes-"

"I want things to work out, too. Trudy. I tried last night when I called her."

The phone call had gone like this.

He had dialed the phone but pushed the end button before he made her phone ring. To put it off ten minutes more, he grabbed his sketchbook and replicated his cell phone except instead of buttons; he drew an old-fashioned rotary dial.

Then, feeling better, he punched in the numbers for his house.

"Hi," he said. "It's me."

"You're calling me pretty late."

"Sally, it's quarter after nine."

"Yep, a time of night where maybe you just got back from a dinner date and are feeling guilty. When was the last time you saw Mercedes?"

"A day ago, while I was at the gallery. Just in passing. All I've been thinking about is you. I really miss you, Sally."

He heard a knife clang against a plate, and he got a mental picture of her sitting on the couch eating saltines with grape jelly. Making a big mess. "Things aren't the same around the house without you here," she admitted. "But I'm sure you think this place is falling apart without you and that simply ain't the case.

"Bobvilla, come lick this off the couch."

"Sally, I really want to work this out."

"That's good to hear. Maybe, I was a little hasty kicking you out. We did need some time alone though. Maybe now, it's time to talk."

"I would like that, Sally. How about tomorrow? I have to pick some paintings up from the shop before heading back to Minneapolis, anyway."

"What?"

"You don't have a problem with me picking up some paintings, do you?"

He heard a crash. Then, "No. Come tomorrow at ten because I won't be here." She clicked the phone off.

Trudy looked into his eyes. "If you want things to work out, try this." Trudy picked up her <u>Men are From Mars, Women are from Venus</u>. "Stop sucking."

Chapter 21 Plaque

They had just finished the mural. Working every day for two weeks, they had come in under budget and ahead of schedule, which had made the board of Minneodyne very pleased. He knew these were the reasons they had been celebrating but couldn't quite get these reasons to cover why he was laying on top of Mercedes with his tongue down her throat.

It had been building up. However, so was the plaque on his teeth and he had not gone to the dentist.

It had been building up. Standing next to her and seeing her soft skin and the turn of her neck. He watched her graceful wrists as she painted and her butt when she leaned over. And then there was the fact she understood his art as well as he did.

"Tomorrow it's back to the real world," she said.

"Don't say that. I'm not ready for the real world again." Then he put his lips on hers. "To go back to not being understood."

Mercedes turned her head out of his kiss and looked at him. Then she smiled a smile Wes didn't quite get.

She moved up to the sweet spot on the bed and his lips followed hers. She got into the ready position and a baseline rally ensued. Dental visits could wait; other build-ups couldn't. An explosion of emotions erupted in him that made him feel justified because Sally had kicked him out. He felt wanted because Mercedes was nibbling on his ear. He felt guilty because his tongue was darting in her mouth. He felt sure he would stop kissing her in a little while. He felt a betrayer because of his vows. He felt her breast with his hand.

His phone rang and Wes lunged for it. As if it rang too many times or if he didn't pick it up, that the caller on the other line would know what he was doing.

"Zip up, Wes," Sally said." I want to talk to you."

"What? What?"

"It's a joke, Wes. I swear you had a sense of humor when I married you. You know, you're alone in a hotel room with a movie on skin-o-max just a credit card charge away." While Sally talked, Wes extricated himself from Mercedes. He had switched sports and his final move was a jump to a standing position like he had just finished his floor routine.

"Yes. I get it. Very funny."

Mercedes teased Wes by pulling at the phone and reaching up his shirt. Wes hopped away in morbid fear of that.

"You seem a little out of breath. Were you watching one of those movies?"

"I just got in. I took the stairs up to my room."

"You're in room 206."

"I'm glad you called me, Sally. I would have called you, but I didn't think you wanted me to." He looked over to Mercedes. She looked like her date's wife had just called. "I I-ah wanted to see how Bobvilla the dog was doing."

"Are you mad at him? Wesley Andrew Story, that you are using his full name? Listen. Jan called me and told me it would be best to have a party about two weeks after your opening to keep people excited and talking about your show. You can't have a party at your studio so she thought we should have one at the house."

"I'm sorry, Sally, that she bothered you."

"I told her yes."

"Will you be there?"

"Do you want me to be there?"

"Do you want to be there?"

At this exchange, Mercedes picked up her shoes, tucked his shirttail back in to leave him in the same condition as she had found him and tiptoed to the door. In the morning, he would find she rode home with Amanda and a note on his windshield that said,

When you are ready...

"Yes. Of course, I want you there."

"Good answer. Because there is no way I'm letting you be there with your little girlfriend."

"She's not my girlfriend."

"She's not there right now?"

"No. God you are so paranoid, Sally."

Chapter 22 Homecoming Party

T*hings are bad*, Wes thought, realizing, home to him was now his studio in Pilsen. He had automatically headed there once he reached Chicago and had to turn around because he wanted to see Sally.

This will be bad. Sally's okay with the party at the house because she is ready to move on and doesn't care anymore. A successful show means we can afford to go our separate ways. Wes thought maybe he should come clean that Mercedes had been in his room. He wanted to come clean because Sally seemed to know already. He told himself, *you can lie to yourself and to your guilt, but not Sally.*

Sally's first pickup that usually just sat in the alley behind her shop was in the driveway. It was a small Isuzu with Isemann Fine Furniture Sally Isemann, Owner printed on the door. *Does the newer truck say Sally Story, Owner?* Wes wondered. *Probably not. She is more John Isemann's daughter than Wesley Story's wife.*

At least she's home. Home in the middle of the day? In the Isuzu? She would never drive that. He pictured the weedy area where the Isuzu usually sat. *Unless she was sneaking away from the shop.*

He took the house quietly, going through the house Don Knotts Ninja style. Expecting to find Sally with her tennis buddy, he opened their bedroom door with his eyes shut.

When he was able to open his eyes, he found the bedroom empty.

Then he realized Bobvila had not met him. *Either the dog is dead, or Sally is walking him. Jesus Christ, he's dead.* Downstairs, he looked out the open patio door. There he saw-

Nancy scooping up dog poop in the back yard. "Hey, Wes, I heard you clod-hopping in there."

Bobvila ran through the shitty lawn and jumped up on Wes. Wes scratched him behind the ears but didn't let the dog jump up on him. "Have you been promoted to dog poop removal?"

Nancy scooped a turd into the garbage can Wes recognized as from the kitchen. "Something like that. I'm just here to let Bobvila out, but I had to make a spot for him to go first. Really it needs to be done, but Sally says she's not doing it; it's your duty."

"I don't remember it being in the wedding vows." Wes sat down on the deck steps. "Sally gets home in a few hours. Why do you need to make a trip out here?"

Nancy leaned on her shovel. "Trudy won't be happy I'm saying something, but I'm really worried about you two. Plus, Sally is making things miserable down at the shop. Not that there wasn't already tension in the air you had to jack hammer your way through. Me and Trudy aren't talking. Tiffany's dad is a good friend of your father-in-law's and is giving both of them shit about working with me. And then there's-"

"I'm sorry, Nancy. I didn't mean for this to happen. Where's Sally?"

"I guess I need to quit stalling, huh?" She picked up the shovel and worked at cleaning the lawn. "She's playing tennis with this Curtis guy that looks like his name should be Biff.

"Then they are going out to dinner."

"So. That's nice." *I lost her. She's sleeping with him. That sleezebag took my wife.*

"She took a duffel bag. To shower at his place after tennis."

It's over. It's over. "T-that doesn't mean anything, Trudy. She gets all sweaty when she plays tennis."

"You guys were going along good," Nancy said working the shovel. "Until she realized it was time for her prediction to come true. Call her

Wes. Tell her not to make a mistake she will regret and that you love her. You need to tell her you will stop leaving town."

Anyone thinking of cheating, he thought, *should not drive from Minneapolis to Chicago. Or they should.* From the twin cities to the Wisconsin border, Wes had entertained how entertaining Mercedes would be. He spent the other six and a half hours regretting what had already happened. "I finished the mural. I'm done leaving."

"Until?"

"Next month." He was not going to go do any murals with a pretty woman anymore. He decided there were things he was going to turn down for Sally. Nevertheless, some trips were unavoidable. "I'm going to be part of a show in New York."

"Tell her you won't go."

He gave Bobvila a pet as the dog nuzzled him. Then he got his cell phone out and punched in Sally's number. "Hi, it's me. I'm back from Minnesota."

"You're late. You told me you would be back yesterday or today."

"How is that- Sally, I'm sure you're busy."

"You caught me taking a water break. I'm playing tennis. With Nancy."

He had his own lie of being with Mercedes during a phone call. Still the words put him in a Frida Kahlo painting. "Will you be home soon? I want to come over and talk."

"I don't think so. Nancy and I have plans."

"Really? Well, when will you be home?"

"Late. It's a lady's night out. I may even crash at Trudy and Nancy's."

The sun began to break through the clouds, and it was suddenly much brighter. His own backyard suddenly foreign to him.

"Wes? Are you still there?"

"Can I come over and get Bobvila." Suddenly he wanted to have something Curtis could not take. "I'm going to be home now and can take care of him all day."

"Well, yeah. He's your dog."

Wes gave a soundless snort. Sally had brought up the idea of a dog, picked him out, and chose his name. Wes was allergic to him and had to take Claritin to be able to live with him.

"I got him to keep you company while you painted. So go pick him up if you want. Where are you?"

"Outside of Chicago."

Chapter 23 Cruel Mistress Fate

The memory of kissing Mercedes got the best of him. Which he *was* going to be bested. Either by the make out session or the fact Sally had been on a date. Wes chose the kissing and the words "When you are ready." After agonizing on what to do all the next day, he called Mercedes and acted as if he was ready.

He assumed that she knew he wasn't.

Over the next couple of days, Wes picked her up after her shift at the gallery at one and they would have lunch and take Bobvila for walks.

They kissed. Perfunctory kisses. A kiss a grandma might acquiesce to because it will get grandpa to leave her alone. They held hands as they walked, and they got along great.

They spent most of the afternoon together until Mercedes would have to run. Usually, she said it was to meet her mother or run an errand for her. For the reasons she gave and for others that he created, Wes decided that the Michael Jan mentioned was a nephew or a kid Mercedes babysat for. Which was a good thing because the baby conversation after Sally's birthday party had freaked him out. Breakfast with Trudy and Nancy's kids the next morning was proof he was not good with kids. Their eating sounds and morning breath told him his own kids would starve to death because he would be unwilling to hear that every morning.

He didn't contemplate anything too deeply. Wes was just happy for the company, so he didn't have to think about Sally. He was happy, too, with the afternoon dates so that he didn't have to turn down a beautiful woman's offer to make love. Certain parts of him were telling him that it would serve Sally right for being on a date. The rest of him knew he would lie awake afterward, and regret betraying both women.

Chapter 24 A Show & Dinner

Wes walked around in his best suit and hard shoes, which changes a man's whole demeanor. He felt confident and powerful and in control of the room. Unfortunately, he was alone while the employees of the gallery were getting things ready for his opening. Even in hard shoes, especially in hard shoes, it was hard to feel powerful in a one-room studio apartment with only a beanbag chair to sit on and a homesick Bobvilla was sacked out on that.

At the gallery, he felt confident. Nervous and confident. Nervous, confident, and alone. When people arrived for the opening night of his exhibition, he stopped being nervous. His suit and hard shoes mingled, broke into groups of people having discussions and contributed, answered questions making good eye contact, and directed potential buyers to the restrooms with accurate directions.

He still felt halved.

Sally would have complained her shoes were hurting her feet. That nobody was paying attention to her. That she had twenty bucks riding on the Bulls and wanted to know the score.

She was supposed to be here.

Mercedes was. Her eyes were always on him to reassure him and at times, they would meet up and discuss how the night was going until they became a couple and stayed together for the rest of the night. When there was nothing else to do for a moment except stand and wait for the next thing to happen, they had each other to make cutting comments about the guests.

Dapper old men in dapper suits and dowdy old men in dowdy suits stood in their own miasma of cologne. Women in bright colors wearing bright red lipstick walked with the men. Weaving in and out of them was Jan in her heels. Saul in his flannel shirt and Amanda in black showed up late. Juan was in a tuxedo, working as a waiter.

Everyone seemed to just be contrast to Mercedes in her pale green top and flower print skirt. He could sense where she was at all times like how you can sense when the cat jumps up on the bed while you're sleeping and walks all over you.

As the night wound down, Mercedes leaned into him. "I'm taking you out tonight to celebrate. We can go to Kristoff's ."

"How about Francesco's?"

She tilted back on her high heels and rubbed his arm. "This is your special night. You get the star treatment."

"I have to stop and let the dog go pee first."

The night was all about him. It was his exhibit opening. He was the reason for being at the gallery and most people spent a large amount of time talking about themselves. People talking to him would throw him in the conversation, but only as a passing comment and then get on to self-veneration. "I am a struggling artist like yourself........I am a great collector of Chicago artists........when I get my own show like you have..........I have had many openings like yours in my twenty-five years and they are still exciting." Worse yet was that the few mentions made of his paintings, which is all he wanted, were wrong. He was heaped with praise over his classic lines and nostalgic tones which none of his paintings had. He was compared to Norman Rockwell. Someone even referred to him as the Ben Affleck of painting and Wes did not take that as a compliment.

And while he wasn't on the verge of crying, he saw crying from where he was. He had pictured the night in his head since he was a teen, but no one got the message of his paintings. Except for Mercedes.

"These idiots," she said, catching his arm and leaning up to his ear conspiratorially. "They don't get your paintings, Wes, because they are not really trying."

She let go of him, but then tiptoed up to his ear again. "The loneliness of love is beautiful. Too beautiful. And you've captured it."

Chapter 25 Our anniversary dinner, bring a date

The restaurant, the one he hated, cheered him up. It was loud and bright, and he walked in with Mercedes who he had noticed the whole night as being sexy. It was womanly sexy, too. Not Amazon, intense, crazy sexy he kept telling himself he did not miss.

The loud and cheerful waitress in her loud and cheerful outfit took their drink orders loudly and cheerfully. It was too much for him because that much cheerfulness meant something would go wrong. That something was wrong, and it gave him a moment of negativity. *I could be suicidal right now. Should be. Tonight, did not go right. My wife is dating someone else. I live in a rat hole and my only piece of furniture is filled with beans.*

He reminded himself he had his own exhibition at a major Chicago art gallery. But it felt like a hollow victory. The bad to good ratio was stacked against him. Like the kids in his playground painting, there was chaos all around and the only thing to do was to stay on the merry-go-round.

He folded his menu and smiled at Mercedes. A smile that dropped like a lead volleyball. Most Saturday nights out, Sally wore one of her Cubs jerseys and got into arguments with White Sox fans at the TGI Fridays. Yet, tonight, she was across the dining room, dressed like she didn't even own a baseball glove.

Without taking his eyes off Sally, he got up and walked over to her as she sat with Curtis. *She has makeup on. She is wearing a Goddamn*

*dress with sequins and her boobs hanging out. And Goddamn heels. For
him, she can wear heels.*

"Sally."

"Oh, hi, Wes."

"Nice of you to dress up. For someone else. Mercedes and I are just
out to grab a bite of something."

"I bet."

"Would you like to join us?"

"No, you and Mazda look cozy."

"How about you? Why are you all dressed up?"

"I haven't done laundry in a while."

"You know why. I needed you at my show tonight."

"You have Mercury."

"Mercedes. Instead, I find you here. I thought you hated this place."

"Why would you think that?"

"Because you say, 'I hate that place every time we drive by it."

"Well, do you like it?"

"No. You know that. You have to be an ass to like this place."

"Hey," Sally's date said. "This is my favorite place."

"Hey," Wes replied. "This is my wife."

"Sally's just my teammate. Chill."

"Please. Coed bar volleyball is just an excuse to get all hot and
sweaty and then get drunk so you can go home with someone and get
the sand out of your underwear."

Sally stared at the wall behind Wes. "Then why did you encourage
me to join up?"

"You needed a hobby. Well, have a terrible night and turn in early.
Finish your drink first though, Biff, because I'm going to phone your
license plate in to the cops when I see you leave."

He walked back to Mercedes and sat down. "Are we ready to
order?"

"Who is that?"

"Ah, my wife."

"I know who she is. Who's the guy she's with?"

"Her boyfriend. Brick Shithouse."

"Well, is..." Mercedes stopped because Sally was standing over them.

"Can I talk to you for a second?"

"Me or Mercedes?"

"Well, I have nothing to say to her. So-"

Wes got up and directed Sally over to the bar. He waved off the bartender and then turned to Sally and stabbed at her with his eyes. He did that to keep them busy because what they wanted to do was caress her naked shoulders.

"She just wants your money, Wes."

"Finally, somebody wants something from me. That's what I want. A woman to rely on me."

"What about me?"

"You never needed me. There is nothing I provide you can't do for yourself. Even now when I'm making it."

"Well, I would take a new truck."

"Really?"

"No. I just bought one. Trudy uses it to deliver furniture while the new guy I hired helps me out."

"Why would Trudy- Trudy and Nancy are still fighting, huh? But they need each other. They will work things out. You seem to be getting along well without me. You even upgraded in the man department with Mr. Muffin over there." He looked her up and down. "You never dressed up like that for me."

"I didn't want to be alone tonight. That's why he's here."

"Isn't that what every relationship is based on? The fear of being alone."

"Wes. What is today?"

"Friday."

"No."

"I'm pretty sure it is."

"It's our wedding anniversary, Wes."

Their anniversary had been in the forefront of his mind since she had kicked him out. However, in the days of getting ready for the gallery opening, he had just forgotten. "I forgot. Otherwise, I would have got you something."

"Don't be sarcastic."

He looked over to Mercedes. All she had meant to him tonight sketched over with one broad stroke of seeing Sally. Then he looked over to Sally's muscle-headed date beading his eyes on the waitress as she walked by. "I wish you had never made that prediction."

Sally put her hand on his arm. "Thanks for that. That sentence is the best anniversary gift you've ever given me."

"I paint your portrait every year."

"For the record, Wes. I don't like that. You are recording how I get older every year. No woman would like that."

Wes threw up his hands up in the air. "You could have told me nine portraits ago."

Sally got off her stool. "You should have known it eight paintings ago." She gave him a squeeze on his forearm and left him.

Mercedes finally broke the silence as they sat in the car in front of her apartment. "Boy you sure got quiet after your little talk with Sally. It ruined your night, Wes, to see her. And it was your night."

"Thank you for tonight. I'm sorry I got quiet."

"Wes, it's still early yet. She was not there for you at your opening. I was. So why don't you be here with me. You'll be glad you did." Then she leaned over to him and kissed him hard. Her fragrance of leather and orange blossoms drove him to caress her face and then drag his fingers feverishly over the nape of her neck.

He felt a definite stirring in his lap. His hands wanted to delve into her clothes and his body wanted to be close to herd. He pulled his hand down her back, pulling her closer. She tugged on his shirttail. He instantly did the same to her. Except her blouse wasn't tucked in. This caused him to yank her shirt past her bra. She liked that. She had his shirttail out and he felt her cool fingers on his back. Those fingers hydroplaned on long nails to his stomach. The receptors in his body said, "I need."

His brain was saying otherwise. *Maybe there is a reason my paintings look cheerful. Maybe happiness is everywhere, but I can't recognize it. Because all I feel right now is depressed and I can't take it.*

"I am not up for it, tonight, Mercedes."

She put a hand between his legs.

"Well, literally I am. But I'm still married, and tonight is my anniversary."

She kissed his cheek then. She was slightly out of breath. "Wes. Wes. I understand. But I won't go on like this. If we are going to continue to see each other, then it has to be real. It has to be based on just the two of us. Okay? People get divorced all the time. She kicked you out. So, we're doing nothing wrong. I don't expect you to stop thinking about Sally right away. But if you are going to be with me, you can't pine away for her." She gave him a quick kiss. "Good night, Wes."

Wes took Bobvila out into the midnight aura of Chicago in his suit and with a plastic grocery bag. The street was quieter than he thought a Chicago street could get. He was sure trouble was lurking nearby. The crime rate of the neighborhood bore that out. However, in the cool air, surrounded by streetlight and brick buildings, he felt as if Chicago was talking to him.

He listened and nodded his head.

He went back upstairs, stretched out a new canvas, and primed it a starch white. He raised his brush up without a plan of what to paint. For the first time in a long time, he wanted to paint. Still, he could not draw a single stroke on the canvas. He had not understood what Chicago had said.

Chicago hadn't understood the problem either. He could have taken how nobody at his own opening had gotten the message of his work. He could take seeing his wife out on a date. What he could not was that Sally, his Sally, wasn't there with him on his big night.

Sally's dad was waiting up for her when she came in the door to her house and attacked her high heels to get them off. "Dad, it was stupid for you to wait up for me."

"With my landlord, it will be another twenty years before my apartment gets painted again, and I have the opportunity to wait up for you."

"In twenty years, you'll be living with me so that I can take care of you."

"You sound like you're looking forward to my being an invalid. How'd the night go, Sal."

"I didn't go." She sat down on the couch. "I was at the door of the gallery with my new dress here with its matching handbag and my fuck-me heels on, but I couldn't do it."

"Wes needed you there."

"I needed to be there, Dad, but I felt I would just be in the way. I'm a big, dumb Amazon and I don't fit in with his crowd. Plus, he's pretty mad at me."

John looked up at his daughter.

"So, I didn't go. I called Curtis and made him take me out to a movie and dinner."

"You should've gone Sal. But I guess no harm done."

"That's when Wes saw us at the restaurant."

"Christ on a cracker, Sal."

"I know. I think I'm destined to ruin my marriage just like mom did."

He shook his head. "Don't make me defend your mother. Because I won't do a very good job of it. However, it takes two people to destroy a marriage. Sure, your mom was selfish. Sure, I provided for her for sixteen years and...Sally you are not your mother, not even close. You are too loyal and giving to do what your mother did."

"I just don't want to hurt Wes."

"Ah, honey. It's a little too late for that."

Chapter 26 Through and through

Three days of loneliness. Wes was too lonely to paint. Or perhaps he felt lonely because he was not painting. Or maybe because of Mercedes, he was no longer alone and therefore had lost his edge to create. He had long stretches of time to contemplate it. His loneliness or his lack of it. All he knew was he was sad and needed to talk to someone.

Instead of sitting in front of his easel as he usually did when he felt lonely, Wes sat in the beanbag chair. On the floor in front of him was the black-and-white TV he had bought at a thrift shop. He had his cell phone in his hand, but the fact Sally had refused to give up the TV in the bedroom made him want to throw the phone at the thirteen-inch set with a digital converter that had cost him three times as much as the TV. For a moment, he tried to figure out the last year Kmart made their own TV.

He tried to figure out what he was feeling. To say he missed Sally would be true. To say she was all he thought about would be a romance novel and a lie. He felt incomplete without her. More accurately, he felt like a portrait artist staring at an empty chair where his model should be. However, he missed Mercedes, too. And she had been there for him. For his exhibition and from the moment they met. Wasn't their relationship easier than his marriage had ever been?

We have these amazing conversations; we have a chemistry. We've taken long walks. Her friends keep asking me if I like her. Wes remembered Junior High. He knew what came next. *Going steady.*

So, he dialed her number. Sally's.

A male's voice came on. "Hello?"

"Curtis?" Wes asked.

"No-" John answered.

Wes had already slammed the end button before John could tell him it was his father-in-law and that his landlord was taking forever to paint his apartment.

Wes had chosen Sally over the logical thing to do, again, as always, and as always, it had frustrated him. He thought of how much time he had spent in high school going to her basketball, volleyball, and track meets. He thought of how he hadn't wanted to move out to the suburbs and only did it to make Sally happy. He did not think about how much he enjoyed going to her games or how much nicer the suburbs were.

Instead, he called Mercedes. Knowing what it meant.

The phone call led to him sitting in his car in front of her apartment the next night and there was no denying he would have to act on his feelings. He did not want to do that. He didn't want to jeopardize his marriage. *All the other guys are doing it,* he decided with the conviction only people with penises could have about the subject. *I was just being a coward when I stopped making out (not stupid or gay or still in love with Sally).* He got out of the car and began walking to Mercedes' apartment. *At some point, I need to move on. She did. Tonight, you do. Without hesitation.*

Then why have you been sitting in the car for the last fifteen minutes?

Shut up, he answered with a resolution only a person with a penis could have. *I deserve this.* Walking up the stairs, he thought of how Mercedes made him feel. It was the fleeting emotion of infatuation, the thrill of a new relationship and the magic of the first kiss-

He cupped his hand to his mouth and blew. *Did I brush before leaving-*

The door opened. "Oh, Wes. There you are. I saw your car come in. I thought you had gotten lost."

"I-I was about to knock."

She kissed him and led him in. *Okay we have kissed. But those were kisses in restaurants and in the car. Tonight, we will be kissing in private. We will probably make out.*

She was in her bathrobe. He couldn't really figure that part out. Unless she wasn't the person he thought she was.

She smiled and extended her hand toward the recliner behind him. Sitting there was a small boy.

"I promised Michael we could go down to the pool tonight." She opened her robe and flashed him her one-piece swimsuit. "Michael, this is my friend Wes."

Wes jumped, bending as he did so in a Crouching Dragon Hidden Tiger sort of way as Michael put his hand out to shake. "Oh, hi," Wes said to him, realizing Jan had been right about the kid and wondering why Mercedes hadn't mentioned him. "Nice to meet you."

Michael was in a pair of Winnie the Pooh swimming trunks. "Nice to meet you."

Run. A voice in his head said. Except it was more than a voice because the person in his head was holding up two fingers in a cross to ward little Michael off.

He's not that bad, Wes told the voice. *And look at his little dupa just out of diapers.*

I'm looking at her tight ass under that robe, the voice replied. *And I still say 'run.'*

Wes roughed out Michael in his head. A small boy only wanting to go swimming with his mother. Unlike himself at that age, where like in his clown painting, he had been bound to his mother's apron strings, this little boy was being asked to share his mother. Wes sat down on the couch to talk to him.

"So little man, you and your mom are going for a quick swim before bed, huh?" He saw Mercedes out of the corner of his eye, smiling at him.

"I got Winnie the Pooh on my swimsuit," Michael said. "You can go to the pool with us."

Wes turned to tell Mercedes he didn't have his suit and found himself alone with the little boy. "Where did your mother go?"

Michael shrugged his shoulders.

"Eeyore was my favorite as a kid."

"He's always sad."

"Just a realist."

Mercedes came out from the back hallway and when he saw her now in a bikini and holding up a pair of male swimming trunks, he jumped up, knocking his knees against the coffee table. His body hit flight or fight mode with the intent on flight when she slowly lowered the trunks, and he got a good look at her chest slung into two triangles and her flat stomach.

"I decided to change suits," she said. "And I brought you one." She came around and draped herself around him. "So, you can go swimming with us." Her last word in his ear just before she drew her lips over his cheek in a way that left the only answer to be yes. Yes, but I can't walk down the hall in my current state. *I deserve this. I deserve Mercedes. It has been three months. Sally has moved on and I have a very hot woman (mother,* the voice corrected) *who has feelings for me.*

"I can't." He noticed his hand had found its way to her abdomen. His hand, he hoped, hadn't fallen in love, but was just searching for stretch marks. His hand, in fact, didn't care about stretch marks, or the small C-section scar. Every painting has its imperfections. His hand was in love. Still, he pulled it back faster than when Sally said the words "Stop it, Wes. I have my period."

"I have to go."

"We have a date."

Wes looked at her body, her brown, smooth skin—the kind he had fantasized about while being with Sally (sometimes). However, it was here, and it scared the hell out of him. Almost as much as Michael scared him. What would she do when she saw his thin frame with its paunch and struggling artist tan? "Ah, yeah, but. I'm only comfortable swimming in my own pool."

"You live in an apartment. And there are no swimming pools in Pilsen."

"I mean the community pool. You cut your feet on the bottom, and it leaves your hair smelling funny, but it's the only pool I've been in for a long time."

"Wes, you look—well, scared."

Wes looked at a spot on the floor away from her beautiful body, which he figured might react in a skin rash in contact with his own. Besides, Michael had run over to his mommy, and so a beautiful body and a ready-made family stood in front of him. "What do I have to be afraid of?" *I haven't even gone near water and already I can feel my testicles shriveling.* "I just have to go."

"Okay," she said.

Wes wanted to ask her why she had a pair of guys swim trunks. Maybe he could be relieved it was a bad reason. However, even bad reasons made him think of eating whipped cream off her stomach. There was a fistfight in the lobby of his mind, but inside the theater, this was the movie playing. Fear won the fight. *I have to get the hell out of here.*

"Michael, go get out two towels, please. And look for your water shoes."

"I don't got no water shoes, Momma."

"Look for them anyway." She went to her door and opened it. "You're missing out on something great, Wes."

"Mercedes-" he started, but then just took his exit.

Chapter 27 Perform a Y-turn ahead

Any male, heterosexual, half-functioning mind knew you don't run away from a half-dressed, beautiful woman. The fact he was still in love with his wife shouldn't have mattered because they were separated and that was clearly a loophole you could drive a penis through.

He drove fast, as if Mercedes was chasing him down the street. *When will I ever have the chance again? Now the situation will only become an embarrassment. Something to haunt me.*

It could've proved to Sally's volleyball buddies that I'm not gay.

Why would I care what those homophobic jerks think? Especially since plenty of gay guys get hit on by pretty women, he argued. *Only gay guys turn them down.* The small satisfaction that Wes felt because he hadn't toyed with Mercedes emotions just for the use of her body made him think,

The universal truth about relationships went through his head and somehow it applied to him and Sally. Still, as inner voices were often stupid, his still spouted, *You turned down that body. Definitely sounds gay.*

After driving until he hit Lake Shore Drive, he turned around. *Does the fact I was just too insecure to seduce her mean I still love my wife?*

Yes, it does. He couldn't put it into words that would convince Sally. He couldn't even explain it to himself. However, it did.

He just knew. He had run because for whatever other reasons, he was also not ready to throw away his fidelity to Sally.

He drove to Oaklawn and parked in front of Sally's house.

The kitchen light came on and Wes noticed the living room light was on but hadn't noticed if it had always been on. Then his cell phone rang.

"You did her, didn't you?"

"No, I didn't. Who do you mean?" He was already forgiving her for being angry because he sounded guilty.

"That's fine, Wes. We are separated. I have someone here with me."

"You do?" For a moment, he pictured Curtis wearing his bathrobe. "I mean, I know. I called this morning, and he picked up the phone."

"That was my dad, stupid. Ah, but, you know, he's really here now. Someone is. Here with me."

Open. Open you frickin' lock. He fumbled with the car door but stopped at the thought of trying to fight a naked man. Stopped, actually, by the thought of getting beat up by a naked man and the view he would have of Curtis standing over him.

He was still going in once he worked up the courage, but on the phone, he heard some rustling and wood hitting wood. Then through the picture window he saw Sally open the curtains to what was clearly (even in the dim light) one of his sport jackets draped around his collapsible easel. Sally had her hand around it and was holding its hat on.

Wes let go of the door handle.

"Maybe I should come in and meet him."

"No, he's mad at you for stalking me. He's so mad he has his back to you."

"Who is that? It's not Curtis. That guy has really narrow shoulders and wide hips. Is that Mr. Jansen, our old driver's ed instructor?"

"It's a guy from- I met."

"I didn't sleep with her, Sally. How did you know I was with, I mean, visited Mercedes tonight?"

"I was guessing." Sally moved, bumping into her date. "You just told me." Wes heard a click and then her date fall forward. "My date is leaving. Out the back door. I want you to go, too."

"Where's his car?"

"Around the block. I don't want a scandal in front of the neighbors."

"Why don't I drive around the block so you can get rid of your date and then we can talk this out? I really want to work things out with you."

"You found out about her kid, didn't you?"

"How do you know she had a kid?"

"I guessed it."

"No, you didn't."

"All those gallery openings and receptions you took me to. While you talked art, what do you think me and the other wives- and by other wives I mean life partners- talked about?"

"So, can I drive around and come back in five minutes?"

"My date is gone."

"Does that mean I can just come in?"

"No, it means I'm by myself. Nothing has changed, Wes."

"Yes, something has. I realized how much I need you."

"You always knew that."

"I mean, I know I want you. Forever."

"Since when?"

Wes switched ears with his cell phone. He had two choices. To say a long time ago or say 30 minutes ago while looking at an almost naked woman. "A few weeks ago."

"And it was such a revelation. It was so important to you that you waited until now?"

Damn. "Can we talk, Sally? Please?"

"No. I can't see a point in it."

"Sally, I am begging to just talk to you. I'm willing to do things differently to make this work."

"And that's a start."

Click

Chapter 28 Jumpin' jacks for my love

Wes got up at five, a first since he moved to Pilsen, and brought his coffee over to his easel. From a drawer, he pulled out his half-finished picture of Montrose Beach. He had felt so mixed the first time they had taken Bobvila there. Sad the dogs had only one place in the city to run free into water, but excited to see Bobvila racing along the sand. He felt those same feelings, but the picture stared back at him and would not draw the events of last night out of his head.

With the realization he needed Sally and that the joy in his life was because of her (contrary to his previous theory that his joy was despite her), he thought he could prime himself to paint again. To hedge his bet, he began with a picture that just needed completing. The dog beach on Montrose Avenue with its great view of the Chicago skyline. After an hour, he stopped. What he wanted to paint was the view of the dog beach as if someone had waded in and turned around. He wanted to put a couple standing on the beach watching their dog jump after a tennis ball in the water.

It had to be a couple standing there. Because that is what he had been when he had experienced it.

How much time have I sat in front of a canvas? How much of my life did I miss as I sat alone painting? His brain amassed confusion and doubt as he stared at the canvas. *What if it's for nothing?*

What if I am not an artist, but just a moron?

Then he had a question that was the answer for him. *Have I spent the time it took to do one landscape on trying to get Sally back? On trying to like what Sally likes?*

The question milled around in his head and then began to seep in like kitten piddle in a litter box until it clumped. *I can be more like who Sally needs.*

He went to the kitchen cupboard where he kept his clothes for lack of a dresser and put on a pair of sweats, his jacket, his gym shoes, and a scarf. *I can be more like Curtis and the rest of the Biff's. I can be more athletic. I can buff out so Sally can see I change. I can spend time doing those athletic things she likes.*

He jogged in place as he waited for the elevator. Then he hit the streets running.

Shit, he thought as he rounded the first corner and hit a wet spot that landed him on his butt. Some hooligans were at the corner and laughed. He struggled to his feet.

"Yo, man. You all right?"

"Good." Wes gulped and took off running on rubber legs until he thought anyone that had seen him fall would no longer see him. He stopped and put his hands on his knees. Running on the slippery, dangerous streets of Pilsen would not improve his health.

He walked around the block and went back to his apartment. He decided he wasn't going running again unless he became suicidal, and the YMCA was out of the question. He envisioned a locker room where he would feel less safe than on the Chicago streets and there would be naked old men. On the running track there would be actual athletic people lapping him as he held his side and leaned on a wall to catch his breath. And he just didn't do treadmills. To him, people on them looked like a row of hamsters on that little Ferris wheel contraption.

Back in his apartment, he tried jogging in place, but it made his windows rattle.

He tried a push-up. Then he tried a sit-up. Then he stayed sat up. He looked around. *What can I do? How can I get into shape the right way?*

It didn't take him long to look around his barren apartment. But his eyes landed on the shelves the last tenant had made out of particle board and cement blocks. Then he looked at his broom and made a homemade barbell.

Sitting on the top shelf were four Michener novels he had gotten at the thrift store after finding out how retro cool watching a black & white TV was not.

He hefted the novels to the floor and duct-taped them to his broom. He did two reps and that felt like enough exercise for the day, so he took to his beanbag chair with an icepack on his hip.

After a while, he went out and bought "Buns of Steel," "Cardio Hip-Hop Workout," and "New York City Ballet Workout."

He also picked up "Totally Nude Aerobics" to counteract the rest of the titles up at the checkout, and because he had been by himself for several months.

Later, he went to the closest Sears to get a DVD player. Then, even later, he went to Walmart to buy an adapter to make the DVD work on his TV and bemoaned the end of Marshall Field's.

At midnight, he went back to Walmart and bought a new TV.

The next morning, he got up at five, but instead of even thinking to paint, he walked in the mall. This seemed right to him because his quest to get Sally back replaced his drive to paint. Too, it boosted his self-esteem to pass up the other mall walkers. They were all over sixty, but he was only a newcomer.

Chapter 28 Crazy for your love

Wes looked out Jan's open door and observed several people looking at his art.

"You know," Jan said, "It would be a good idea for you to go out there."

"I can't."

"You can't?"

"No. Mercedes is out there."

"You can't just avoid her forever."

"I can. I've been here every day this week and I haven't seen her."

"That's because Mercedes hides in the back when she sees you come in and we don't even have a back."

"Well, that's silly. She doesn't need to do that. I'll do all the hiding."

"Wes, are you alright? You look terrible."

"Actually, I feel good. I've been exercising every day. All day."

"You got a club membership down at the Y, then. Your hands aren't rough and cracking, so I know you're not running outside."

"The Y? Jan. What am I going to do there? Swim laps? I've yet to see a kid at a pool get out and go to the bathroom. I walk here every morning and then twice a day I run down the stairs to get the newspaper and the mail and then back up. For lunch, I make myself a large glass of raw eggs."

"And you drink that, Wes?"

"No," he said. "I always plan to, but I can't bring myself to do it, so I mix in some mushrooms and cheese and fry up myself a Frittata. It should work out the same, shouldn't it? I have this strict regime of exercising and I feel really good. Today, I'm pretty sore, so I just worked out to "Stretching for Seniors" twice, but tomorrow I'm back to "Eagle Claw Kung Fu- The Workout" six times a day."

Jan leaned back in her chair. "And your mental health?"

"I think I really just kinda answered that. But I've figured out I have to bring balance into my life. I have to make time for Sally's interests as well as painting."

"So, how is painting going, then?

"I haven't painted in months."

"Well, at least you're back together with Sally."

"Haven't seen her in weeks."

"Wes, I think your cheese has slipped off your cracker."

"Oh, absolutely. I think that's how Sally wants me."

Chapter 29 Like a Bat out of Hell

Getting the house ready for the party had been tense for Wes. Sally had been helpful and calm, and that was not like her at all. He had tried to talk to her. Then he tried to thank her. He even tried to fight with her, but she kept too busy to get involved with anything he had to say.

The first time they made eye contact was when the doorbell rang for their first guests, and they went to the door together.

Wes opened the door to Nancy and Trudy. "We're so happy to see you," he said, hugging both.

"Finally," Sally said. "Somebody I can at least talk to."

"We're here for the free liquor, boss. Point the way."

Sally hugged them both and pointed the way. "Why haven't Wes and I had you two over in so long?" The three of them stopped and looked at her with furrowed brows. She had the same look. "I mean, it's good to see you two. Together."

"The same," Trudy answered.

"Thanks to you guys," Nancy managed.

Sally folded her arms. "I told Wes it was important to watch the kids for you."

Trudy unfolded her arms and took Sally's hands. "It wasn't that. We, however, watched you two and didn't want to end up so pathetic. Sally. Wes. We finally figured out what we needed was time like tonight where we make time for only each other. To make everything else fall into place, we have to put our relationship first. So, if the other person is fucking up the kids, so be it."

Nancy winked. "Drinking is our second priority tonight, though."

A bunch of people came in and Sally played bartender at their makeshift bar. "Tell me again why I am doing this?"

"This party is to keep the interest going in my exhibit. You agreed to let the party be here because I live in a rathole, and you are the one responsible for that."

"Listen, Buster. I'll play the loving wife for your nerdy friends, but I reserve the right to disappear upstairs whenever I'm needed and to be obnoxious when I should make myself scarce."

"Just like old times, then," Wes allowed.

"Good one, Wes. I must remember to tell that to my lawyer."

"Diane and Joe. Welcome," she called out to the couple standing in front of the screen door.

"Hi, Sally. You must be busy with your own art. The last couple of functions, Wes came solo."

Sally shot Wes a "you're lucky" look. "Yeah, building my furniture keeps me busy. Otherwise, nothing, and I mean nothing, would keep me away from the art community's social life."

"Like at our party a few weeks ago," Diane said. "Wes wouldn't have been able to play The Newlywed game if Mercedes hadn't been there to be his partner. Can you believe they won?"

"Somebody mention me?" Mercedes said from outside the screen door.

Sally looked at Mercedes' strapless little black dress and went to lock the door. Moving fast, Mercedes pulled it open. "Well, speak of the devil and look at what the cat dragged in. Come here. Give old Sally a hug."

Sally swung her long arms around Mercedes and whispered. "Go near my husband and I will kill you."

"I'll try to keep him away," she answered in a normal voice. "But I rode here with Diane and Joe, and they have to leave early. I may need a ride back home. Maybe with Wes seeing as he lives just around the corner now."

Sally re-tightened her hug. "I'm serious. I'll build you a coffin and bury you before your body gets cold."

"I'm going to go get a drink now. I'm so glad your husband invited me." Mercedes pried herself away from Sally.

"Oh, Wes, dear." Sally went to hug him next. She caught his arm and spun him away from the next group of guests to arrive. "I need to talk to you about the veggie tray." She pulled him over to it.

"Yes? What about the veggie tray? Oh, we have too much green. We need some contrasting-"

"Shut up. What is she doing here? And why when I grabbed your arm did I feel tone there?"

"I've been working out." *For you.* Wes wanted to say it. It just didn't come out.

"Great. That's what divorced guys do when they want to put themselves back out on the market."

"I am making myself the person you want me to be. Doesn't that mean anything to you?"

"If it was true, then maybe. But her presence here tells me it's not."

"She's representing the gallery, Sally. Jan's out of town. People would wonder why no one from the gallery was here. Besides, it doesn't matter. She hates me. And actually, I need to go over there and take my lumps."

"Fine. Go take lumps. Just as long as you both end up miserable."

"Be back in a second, dear."

"Sarcasm with the 'dear?'"

"No. Remember, I want to get back together with you. Remember me outside in my car begging to come in?"

"Oh, manipulative, then." She noticed Wes wasn't going to spar back. He was just staring at her. "Go take your lumps."

Mercedes had a drink and was attempting to drown ice cubes with her swizzle stick. She knew many of the guests from the art community but was standing by herself.

She held up her glass as Wes came over. "Just soda. Michael wakes up early."

"I'm glad you came. I think you're going to have a miserable time."

"Well. Thanks for that."

Wes stuffed his hands into his pockets. "I mean. I'm sorry about the other night. I'm going through a rough time and have been really unfair to you."

"It's okay." She looked at him and then back down at her drink. "I'm used to guys seeing a five-year-old responsibility and running in fear."

"I guess that's what I did."

"It's literally what you did. It's why I didn't ever mention Michael. I wanted you to get attached to me before finding out I'm a package deal. I guess it never actually works, but most guys find me desirable enough to stick around long enough to trick my son into liking them so they can sleep with me. So, thank you for not finding me desirable."

"That's just it. You're beautiful. Too beautiful."

Mercedes laughed a laugh that caused a kitchen cabinet to be slammed shut. "And it's you, not me, right?"

"Exactly."

"I thought you'd be more creative. Don't you have some fresher lines?"

Wes clutched her arm. "Don't say that. I don't have pickup lines. Just loyalty ones. I was really drawn to you, kid, or no kid. Although the kid did really freak me out. But besides the image of you seeing me naked and realizing you made a mistake; I saw how much it would hurt Sally when she found out.

"And I also saw how hurt you would be when you realized that I still love my wife. You're my friend, Mercedes. I do care about you, and I think you have feelings for me."

"Whatever gave you that idea?"

"I'm not used to people wanting me. I notice it when it happens."

"I know of three guys here that want you."

"And Mercedes, I'm not used to having feelings for someone other than my wife. I needed you and I wanted you."

"But you ain't ever gonna love me? But don't be sad? Cause two out of three ain't bad?"

"No. I do, or at least I could really fall for you. Despite you quoting a Meatloaf song. But I am still in love with my wife, so all that means is I would keep stringing you along, using you for emotional support, but never giving you what you need."

"And I've kicked guys' asses for that. Literally." She reached over and kissed his cheek. "Thanks, Wes. I'll probably hate you by the time I get home tonight and sort that out, so I wanted to thank you now."

Sally saddled up behind him when Mercedes walked away. "Laughing. A kiss on the cheek and a sweet grin on your face. How will you recover from taking your lumps?"

"You know what, Sally, you pushed me towards her. You made me make a fool out of myself just so you won't hate me during our divorce proceedings. I had hoped this party would help us reconcile, but I don't think I can fake our togetherness for one more moment."

"Well, I certainly can't."

A man tapped them on the shoulders. "Excuse me. Jan Hutchinson directed me to come to this party tonight. I want to do a story on you two for the Tribune. Really focus on the whole husband and wife working in their own mediums, but with a common passion for beauty angle. What do you say?"

"Okay. But the main focus should be on me," they said in unison.

Chapter 30 Through the tunnel of love

Wes walked into his studio, pulled his stool to the middle of the room, and sat down in the darkness. For a moment, he sat and let the events of the night paint him. He was red and pink, swirled in delicate strokes from Mercedes. He was electric blue thinking about the article and what it meant to his career. He was puddles of watercolors thinking about Sally. He had definitely felt something to spend time with her. It made him feel warm and desert orange, yet cold and coal black that she was being angry and stubborn.

Then he rolled out his easel and his paints and pulled out his emotions and arranged them on his pallet. He had a canvas ready. He had prepared it weeks before, but his block had not let him paint.

He sat, worrying his paint and emotions would dry out before he painted anything. The blank canvas became more ominous with each passing minute, and he felt so much, but couldn't get it out.

His phone rang on the counter by his keys. "Yeah, I'm still cleaning up," Sally said into the phone.

"Sorry," Wes said, saying only one word to cover his crying.

"I just thought you would want to know that."

Wes moved the phone from his mouth and breathed deeply. "I thought everything was picked up. You said you'd do the dishes in the morning."

"I'm doing them now. I couldn't sleep."

"So why did you call me?"

"Because I wanted to." Wes heard her tinkle some wine glasses as she sat one on the drying rack. "That's a good reason, isn't it?"

"I don't know."

"Well, think about it, Wes. It is." She hung up.

Wes pushed the end button hard and stomped back to the stool. He began painting the Lower Wacker Drive. It had scared him as a kid. The first time he had gone on it, his family had just moved to Chicago and hadn't even known about the double-decker road built so cars would drive on top and trucks and thru traffic on the road below. It had been late at night and his dad, new to driving in Chicago, had ended up in the dark underground world with its green lights.

This painting would be dark. Only dark.

Tiffany and Jessica were actually washing the glasses. Sally put the phone down and went in search of more. She found her dad on the edge of the couch watching a re-broadcast of a Cubs game while Trudy and Nancy were doing body shots on themselves.

"Dad, I thought you had gone home hours ago."

"I was in your bedroom watching TV."

"You didn't look for the remote in the nightstand, did you?"

"I don't channel surf. I pick a show and stick with it."

"Of course, you do, dad. Actually, I'm glad you are here. I need someone to drive the girls home."

John turned the game off. "About that. I don't think they should be here."

"Why, dad? Because there are drunken lesbians here and you have a problem with them?" She looked over at Trudy pouring tequila into Nancy's belly button with her T-shirt pulled up and set the bottle on Nancy's chest. "Actually, you too, knock that off."

"As their boss, you need to look out for those young girls."

"They chose to come here. I don't even think their parents would be upset. In fact, I'm sure they wouldn't."

The doorbell rang. And just in case her math was a little off on that, Sally backed away from the front door. "Would you get that, Dad?"

John opened the door to Tiffany's dad, who had the screen door open and barged in. "What the hell John? She said she was with her boyfriend, but I know she's here. Hanging out with dykes and faggots. You go fruity too, John? You a blanket-biter? Tiffany, get your ass out here." Without waiting for her ass or the rest of her, he ran up the stairs to the bedrooms and then came back down. He looked at Trudy and Nancy. "What did you do with my daughter, you carpet munching whores."

"Stop," John called out. "Carl, you stop right now."

"You're not going to stand up for these perverts, are you?"

"Keep a civil tongue or I will throw you out on your ass. At the shop, you had the legal right to take your daughter. But you will not talk to my friends that way. Do you understand me?"

"I understand you're taking sides with the queers."

John walked over to him, grabbed his shirt, and pulled him towards the door. Carl took a few swings, but John caught his fist each time and forced it back down. Carl's jowly face turned red and twisted in anger. John's face was redder. He breathed through his nose and his head shook. "I am on the side of good people, and I will not allow you to talk about anyone like that," he said and then dragged Carl through the house. On the front steps, John flung him down to the ground. "You were warned."

"I ain't leaving without my daughter."

John went and knelt by Tiffany's father. "This is what is going to happen. You have been drinking, so I am going to drive you and Tiffany home. Then I'm going to wake Sue up and tell her what an ass you've been."

John walked back into the house and three heads snapped towards him. "I'm going to take the girls home now. Nancy and Trudy, I'm sorry I didn't stand up for you the first time."

Sally stopped him before he got to the kitchen, where Tiffany and Jessica were still hiding. "Thanks, Dad. But I hope you didn't ruin a friendship just for us. At the shop you didn't-"

"That's the great thing about life, Sal. Something your mom never understood. In life, there is almost always a chance to correct any mistake you made. You take the wrong path and there's always a way to jump on the path you want." He touched her face.

JUST AFTER SUNRISE, Wes put his brush down. He had painted, and he had thought of Sally's phone call. There had been plenty of times he had been hurt by Sally during their marriage. However, she had never done it intentionally. So, she didn't do it now either. Her calling meant she still wanted their marriage.

The sunless Lower Wacker Drive was his world without Sally. He picked up a new brush and touched new paint to the canvas. He had to put Sally in it.

Chapter 31 Rabbet Unglued

John was cutting a rabbet with a router on a raw picture frame when Sally came over and stood in front of him. He looked up and powered the tool down.

"Since when have we made picture frames?"

"It's a special project. For Wes."

"Oh, you talk to him?"

"I don't not talk to him. I think this picture frame is for a present for you."

"Great. Another portrait that shows that to him I'm only a subject. Something to be painted like a bowl of fruit. Framed up with my own wood."

"What can I do for you, Honey?"

"Well, actually. It has to do with Wes. A reporter wants to do a big article on us. Taking the whole two diverse people but both artistic angle."

John felt the edge of his rabbets with his thumb. "Don't you think you should decide if you and Wes are, in fact, together?"

Sally handed him a square of sandpaper off the table. John sanded a small burr. "I can't worry about that right now. I want that article to show people how you've been my inspiration."

"No. I'm not going to be included in any article. Sal gal, don't look like that."

"I want you to have the attention you deserve."

"It sounds to me like this article is supposed to be about you and Wes." John put his safety glasses back on, but Sally placed her hand on his arm.

"I want you to get the attention you deserve. Finally."

"Sally. I'm proud of you and I wouldn't trade my shifts at the shop for anything. But I thought that by now you knew I was okay." He couldn't help but to tighten his jaw. "You always tried to give me the love your mom didn't. And I guess I needed it because I let it go on for so long. But if you want to work things out with Wes, then you need to focus on Wes. And yourself. Focus on yourself. But Wes, too. You should be working on Wes's happiness. That kid is losing it. He looked like he had been up for 48 hours."

"Dad."

"And your own. Never forget about you own happiness." John studied his rabbets again. "Don't ask me how any relationship works. Because you must put yourself first so you don't lose yourself and yet the secret of happiness is to do for others." He sanded at the long-gone burr.

"I guess what I'm saying is make your life with someone you love but remember to have lunch with your dad sometimes."

Sally looked down at her work boots for a moment. "God, you are getting all preachy."

"I want you to be happy, Sally." Sally took up one side of the future picture frame and studied the rabbet on it. He took it back. Looked at her. "So, go talk to Wes."

She shook her head. "It's too late to talk. I need something from him."

"A sign?"

"I don't know. Maybe."

"Then what Sally? If you don't know, then how can he?"

"I heard what you said last night. I just need something, Dad. I don't know what it is. Something to know that he isn't complete without me."

John looked at her. "Not complete? Have you talked to him lately? He's completely unglued."

Chapter 32 Wahoo for hoohoo

The photographer snapped a picture of Sally at the lathe, sawdust in her hair and her safety glasses on her forehead. A few fine particles danced in the air around her, having been tossed up by Trudy a few moments before.

The tour of the home and of Sally's shop had gone well. The photographer had gotten her pictures and Miriam, the reporter, hadn't asked any hard questions. "Now, where is your work studio, Wes?" asked Miriam, looking up from her notebook where she had just scribbled down a quote from Tiffany. Sally has taught me so much about life, love, and applying varnish. Oh, thank God my dad never reads your magazine. "We got some wonderful shots of you and Sally at your beautiful kitchen table. And Sally with her coworkers. We just need a few of you at work.

"Actually, that room above your garage would make a great studio."

Wes leaned on the front counter to Sally's shop. "I have a studio in Pilsen. I like to be in the art district."

"Aren't you afraid with all that crime?"

"Terrified. I mean, no. Not at all."

"Okaay. Let's go there and get a few pictures."

"Let's stay here," Sally suggested. "We could get a few shots of me with my dad."

John, standing with the rest of her crew at the front of the store, shook his head. Wes standing next to her, nodded his head. "Yeah. We don't want to see my studio. Big empty room with canvases and art supplies. Lots of art supplies. There's nothing out of the ordinary to see there. Nothing at all."

"I have to see it, Wes. It wouldn't be a story without it. You're rising status is the reason we are doing the story." Wes shot Sally a smug look. "You are finally coming into your own after Sally being respected for her wonderful furniture for so long." Sally shot him a eat feces and die look.

Wes folded his hands in front of him. "Yes. My wife's art has long inspired me." He smiled at her and touched her arm. "And she has made a beautiful environment for us to live in. When I'm not there, I miss it terribly."

"Let's go take some pictures of Wes's studio," Sally said. And when Wes saw Sally meant it, he was too touched to speak. He was also too touched to think of what waited for them.

He thought about worrying as they drove to his studio. He could run up ahead and try to throw the messed-up way he was living into the courtyard, but Sally and Wes rode with Miriam while John, Nancy, and Jan followed in the company truck.

Panic set in Wes as they climbed the stairs. He gave a glance at Nancy, who had visited him and knew how he lived and received a shrug. He was tired of thinking lesbians had all the answers. He unlocked his door and swung it open.

The first thing about the room was that it was bare. The hardwood floor could have been a dance studio instead of an art studio.

"Why aren't there any pictures?" Miriam asked, dropping her notepad.

Jan spoke up. "He's going to have an exhibit at an art gallery in New York."

"The rest he put on eBay," Nancy added.

"The online auction where they sell used toys and purses?"

Wes ignored the question because he was studying Sally as she stepped to the middle of the room.

"It's performance art," Jan said with no hint she had no idea what Wes was doing. "He is making a statement by selling them over the Internet."

"Performance for whom?"

"People that read his blog."

Sally looked at him. "You have a blog?"

"I will as soon as I buy a computer." Wes answered, following Sally. "I want to stop being so isolated from the world."

Miriam wandered the apartment as the photographer audited the room with her camera. "Are you going to paint this?" Miriam asked, pointing to his four Michener books duct-taped to the broom.

"No, but I can do fifty reps with them."

"It's pretty dark in here for a studio," Miriam said to nobody. That was the second thing noticeable about the apartment. Wes had garbage bags taped over his windows to keep the glare off his TV so he could do his workouts.

Wes hesitated and kept Sally in his line of vision. She clearly looked disturbed at how he was living. His TV and DVD player were on the cinderblock shelves. He had an old exercise bike, one with a spoke tire, in one corner and an air mattress he used as a bed in another corner. "Well, mostly I'm concentrating on Sweatin' to the Oldies and doing reps with the books. I also lie on the mat over there and do the Thigh-Master and the *Abs of Steel* video three times a day."

"More performance art for a nonexistent audience?" Miriam asked, motioning to the photographer to put his camera away.

"No, just building up my biceps so I can get a barbed-wire tattoo. I haven't painted in several months or received payment for my mural yet. I've been selling painting on eBay in order to live. I mean, pay the rent on my studio."

Sally, in her slow progression, had made it to his easel.

"You seem to have a painting under that tarp on your easel," Miriam said, following behind Sally and stopping to retrieve her notebook.

"That's not a painting. No painting here."

"It's flat, square and sitting on an easel."

"The truth is I haven't been painting."

"A painter that doesn't paint doesn't make it into my magazine."

"Well, of course, it's a painting. It's just not finished, and a painter never reveals his work until it's finished. It's called integrity."

Miriam flipped her notebook closed.

Before Wes caved, Sally yanked the tarp and uncovered her painting. It was the dark and damp Lower Wacker Tunnel, but beaming out bright yellow-orange light was Sally as Botticelli's Venus coming forth out of the darkness of the tunnel on a shell. Her hair was long and flowing, but completely gray. Her face was of the thirty-year-old Sally and her body was how he remembered it the last time they made love. On the robe about to be draped over her was a tapestry of other paintings of his. The dirty children playing on the playground. God's sunset painting. The portrait he had painted for her their first anniversary. His tribute paintings of Chicago. He had painted the abandoned and haunted graveyard Bachelor's Grove. The Bleacher Bums at Wrigley Field. The unfinished Dog Beach picture.

The photographer took in the picture over Sally's shoulder as Sally stood motionless for a long time. Nancy stood in the doorway with John. She wanted to see the picture, too, but from what she could see, John was looking everywhere except at the nude picture of his daughter. She stayed by him to keep him company.

Wes picked up his canvas tarp off the floor. He brought himself to look at Sally. "Sorry, I-"

Sally reached over and grabbed his arm. "No. I get it. You love Chicago and painting it because it represents me. And you love me." She kissed him and embraced him. He kissed her back. The photography clicked away, but they stood holding each other. He wanted to tell her how she was his muse. Everything he painted was to show Sally to the world and show Sally how textured and deep his love was for her. She was everything to him, the good, the bad, the happy, the things that hurt his heart but made him feel alive. However, he kept his mouth shut. She had gotten it.

"Thank you for having my arm cover both breasts," Sally said, looking at him. "But my hoohoo is right out there."

"I like your hoohoo."

"See, Wes. I'm a simple girl. That means a lot to me."

"The one thing you are not," Wes said. He and Sally were now holding each other in a slow spinning dance around the room. "Is simple."

Don't miss out!

Visit the website below and you can sign up to receive emails whenever Thomas Cannon publishes a new book. There's no charge and no obligation.

https://books2read.com/r/B-A-NLFBB-LLYPC

BOOKS 2 READ

Connecting independent readers to independent writers.

About the Author

Thomas Cannon was raised on a small dairy farm near Spencer, Wisconsin. While drawn to the honest work of farming, he followed a passion for writing and graduated with a bachelor's degree in English from the University of Wisconsin- Stevens Point. In August 2021, he was named the Poet Laureate of Oshkosh. Author of many short stories and poems, he is dedicated to growing his local writing community. Each year he helps to organize the Lakefly Writers Conference and co-hosts Author Showcase on the Oshkosh Media Channel. He and his wife have raised three children and have two grandchildren.

Read more at https://thomascannonauthor.com/.

Milton Keynes UK
Ingram Content Group UK Ltd.
UKHW040708201123
432908UK00001B/205